MORA

THE NGHI OF FEAR

KATHERINE DALTON RENOIR ('Moray Dalton') was born in Hammersmith, London in 1881, the only child of a Canadian father and English mother.

The author wrote two well-received early novels, *Olive in Italy* (1909), and *The Sword of Love* (1920). However, her career in crime fiction did not begin until 1924, after which Moray Dalton published twenty-nine mysteries, the last in 1951. The majority of these feature her recurring sleuths, Scotland Yard inspector Hugh Collier and private inquiry agent Hermann Glide.

Moray Dalton married Louis Jean Renoir in 1921, and the couple had a son a year later. The author lived on the south coast of England for the majority of her life following the marriage. She died in Worthing, West Sussex, in 1963.

MORAY DALTON MYSTERIES
Available from Dean Street Press

MORAY DALTON

THE NIGHT OF FEAR

With an introduction by Curtis Evans

DEAN STREET PRESS

Published by Dean Street Press 2019

Copyright © 1931 Moray Dalton

Introduction Copyright © 2019 Curtis Evans

All Rights Reserved

Published by licence, issued under the UK Orphan Works
Licensing Scheme.

First published in 1931 by Sampson Low

Cover by DSP

ISBN 978 1 912574 89 6

www.deanstreetpress.co.uk

LOST GOLD FROM A GOLDEN AGE

The Detective Fiction of Moray Dalton
(Katherine Mary Deville Dalton Renoir,
1881-1963)

"GOLD" COMES in many forms. For literal-minded people gold may be merely a precious metal, physically stripped from the earth. For fans of Golden Age detective fiction, however, gold can be artfully spun out of the human brain, in the form not of bricks but books. While the father of Katherine Mary Deville Dalton Renoir may have derived the Dalton family fortune from nuggets of metallic ore, the riches which she herself produced were made from far humbler, though arguably ultimately mightier, materials: paper and ink. As the mystery writer Moray Dalton, Katherine Dalton Renoir published twenty-nine crime novels between 1924 and 1951, the majority of which feature her recurring sleuths, Scotland Yard inspector Hugh Collier and private inquiry agent Hermann Glide. Although the Moray Dalton mysteries are finely polished examples of criminally scintillating Golden Age art, the books unjustifiably fell into neglect for decades. For most fans of vintage mystery they long remained, like the fabled Lost Dutchman's mine, tantalizingly elusive treasure. Happily the crime fiction of Moray Dalton has been unearthed for modern readers by those industrious miners of vintage mystery at Dean Street Press.

Born in Hammersmith, London on May 6, 1881, Katherine was the only child of Joseph Dixon Dalton and Laura Back Dalton. Like the parents of that admittedly more famous mistress of mystery, Agatha Christie, Katherine's parents hailed from different nations, separated by the Atlantic Ocean. While both authors had British mothers, Christie's father was American and Dalton's father Canadian.

Laura Back Dalton, who at the time of her marriage in 1879 was twenty-six years old, about fifteen years younger than her husband, was the daughter of Alfred and Catherine Mary Back. In her early childhood years Laura Back resided at Valley House, a lovely regency villa built around 1825 in Stratford St. Mary, Suffolk, in the heart of so-called "Constable Country" (so named for the fact that the great Suffolk landscape artist John Constable painted many of his works in and around Stratford). Alfred Back was a wealthy miller who with his brother Octavius, a corn merchant, owned and operated a steam-powered six-story mill right across the River Stour from Valley House. In 1820 John Constable, himself the son of a miller, executed a painting of fishers on the River Stour which partly included the earlier, more modest incarnation (complete with water wheel) of the Back family's mill. (This piece Constable later repainted under the title *The Young Waltonians*, one of his best known works.) After Alfred Back's death in 1860, his widow moved with her daughters to Brondesbury Villas in Maida Vale, London, where Laura in the 1870s met Joseph Dixon Dalton, an eligible Canadian-born bachelor and retired gold miner of about forty years of age who lived in nearby Kew.

Joseph Dixon Dalton was born around 1838 in London, Ontario, Canada, to Henry and Mary (Dixon) Dalton, Wesleyan Methodists from northern England who had migrated to Canada a few years previously. In 1834, not long before Joseph's birth, Henry Dalton started a soap and candle factory in London, Ontario, which after his death two decades later was continued, under the appellation Dalton Brothers, by Joseph and his siblings Joshua and Thomas. (No relation to the notorious "Dalton Gang" of American outlaws is presumed.) Joseph's sister Hannah wed John Carling, a politician who came from a prominent family of Canadian brewers and was later knighted for his varied public services, making him Sir John and his wife Lady Hannah. Just how Joseph left the family soap and candle business to prospect for gold is currently unclear, but sometime in the 1870s, after fabulous gold rushes at Cariboo and Cassiar, British Columbia and the Black Hills of South Dakota, among other locales, Joseph left Canada and carried his riches with him to London, England, where for a time he enjoyed life as a gentleman of leisure in one of the great metropolises of the world.

Although Joshua and Laura Dalton's first married years were spent with their daughter Katherine in Hammersmith at a villa named Kenmore Lodge, by 1891 the family had moved to 9 Orchard Place in Southampton, where young Katherine received a private education from Jeanne Delport, a governess from Paris. Two decades later, Katherine, now 30 years old, resided with her parents at Perth Villa in the village of Merriott, Somerset, today about an eighty miles' drive west of Southampton. By this time Katherine had published, under the masculine-sounding pseudonym of Moray Dalton (probably a gender-bending play on "Mary Dalton") a well-received first novel, *Olive in Italy* (1909), a study of a winsome orphaned Englishwoman attempting to make her own living as an artist's model in Italy that possibly had been influenced by E.M. Forster's novels *Where Angels Fear to Tread* (1905) and *A Room with a View* (1908), both of which are partly set in an idealized Italy of pure gold sunlight and passionate love. Yet despite her accomplishment, Katherine's name had no occupation listed next it in the census two years later.

During the Great War the Daltons, parents and child, resided at 14 East Ham Road in Littlehampton, a seaside resort town located 19 miles west of Brighton. Like many other bookish and patriotic British women of her day, Katherine produced an effusion of memorial war poetry, including "To Some Who Have Fallen," "Edith Cavell," "Rupert Brooke," "To Italy" and "Mort Homme." These short works appeared in the *Spectator* and were reprinted during and after the war in George Herbert Clarke's *Treasury of War Poetry* anthologies. "To Italy," which Katherine had composed as a tribute to the beleaguered British ally after its calamitous defeat, at the hands of the forces of Germany and Austria-Hungary, at the Battle of Caporetto in 1917, even popped up in the United States in the "poet's corner" of the *United Mine Workers Journal*, perhaps on account of the poem's pro-Italy sentiment, doubtlessly agreeable to Italian miner immigrants in America.

Katherine also published short stories in various periodicals, including *The Cornhill Magazine*, which was then edited by Leonard Huxley, son of the eminent zoologist Thomas Henry Huxley and father of famed writer Aldous Huxley. Leonard Huxley obligingly read over--and in his words "plied my scalpel upon"--Katherine's second novel, *The Sword of Love*, a romantic adventure saga set in the Florentine Republic at the time of Lorenzo the Magnificent and the infamous Pazzi Conspiracy, which was published in 1920. Katherine writes with obvious affection for

il bel paese in her first two novels and her poem "To Italy,"
which concludes with the ringing lines

> Greece was enslaved, and Carthage is but dust,
> But thou art living, maugre [i.e., in spite of] all thy
>   scars,
> To bear fresh wounds of rapine and of lust,
> Immortal victim of unnumbered wars.
> Nor shalt thou cease until we cease to be
> Whose hearts are thine, beloved Italy.

The author maintained her affection for "beloved Italy"
in her later Moray Dalton mysteries, which include sym-
pathetically-rendered Italian settings and characters.

Around this time Katherine in her own life evidently
discovered romance, however short-lived. At Brighton in
the spring of 1921, the author, now nearly 40 years old,
wed a presumed Frenchman, Louis Jean Renoir, by whom
the next year she bore her only child, a son, Louis Anthony Laurence Dalton Renoir. (Katherine's father seems to
have missed these important developments in his daughter's life, apparently having died in 1918, possibly in the
flu pandemic.) Sparse evidence as to the actual existence
of this man, Louis Jean Renoir, in Katherine's life suggests that the marriage may not have been a successful
one. In the 1939 census Katherine was listed as living
with her mother Laura at 71 Wallace Avenue in Worthing, Sussex, another coastal town not far from Brighton,
where she had married Louis Jean eighteen years earlier;
yet he is not in evidence, even though he is stated to be
Katherine's husband in her mother's will, which was pro-
bated in Worthing in 1945. Perhaps not unrelatedly, em-
pathy with what people in her day considered unorthodox

sexual unions characterizes the crime fiction which Katherine would write.

Whatever happened to Louis Jean Renoir, marriage and motherhood did not slow down "Moray Dalton." Indeed, much to the contrary, in 1924, only a couple of years after the birth of her son, Katherine published, at the age of 42 (the same age at which P.D. James published her debut mystery novel, *Cover Her Face*), *The Kingsclere Mystery*, the first of her 29 crime novels. (Possibly the title was derived from the village of Kingsclere, located some 30 miles north of Southampton.) The heady scent of Renaissance romance which perfumes *The Sword of Love* is found as well in the first four Moray Dalton mysteries (aside from *The Kingsclere Mystery*, these are *The Shadow on the Wall*, *The Black Wings* and *The Stretton Darknesse Mystery*), which although set in the present-day world have, like much of the mystery fiction of John Dickson Carr, the elevated emotional temperature of the highly-colored age of the cavaliers. However in 1929 and 1930, with the publication of, respectively, *One by One They Disappeared*, the first of the Inspector Hugh Collier mysteries and *The Body in the Road*, the debut Hermann Glide tale, the Moray Dalton novels begin to become more typical of British crime fiction at that time, ultimately bearing considerable similarity to the work of Agatha Christie and Dorothy L. Sayers, as well as other prolific women mystery authors who would achieve popularity in the 1930s, such as Margery Allingham, Lucy Beatrice Malleson (best known as "Anthony Gilbert") and Edith Caroline Rivett, who wrote under the pen names E.C.R. Lorac and Carol Carnac.

For much of the decade of the 1930s Katherine shared the same publisher, Sampson Low, with Edith Rivett, who published her first detective novel in 1931, although Rivett moved on, with both of her pseudonyms, to that rather more prominent purveyor of mysteries, the Collins Crime Club. Consequently the Lorac and Carnac novels are better known today than those of Moray Dalton. Additionally, only three early Moray Dalton titles (*One by One They Disappeared*, *The Body in the Road* and *The Night of Fear*) were picked up in the United States, another factor which mitigated against the Dalton mysteries achieving long-term renown. It is also possible that the independently wealthy author, who left an estate valued, in modern estimation, at nearly a million American dollars at her death at the age of 81 in 1963, felt less of an imperative to "push" her writing than the typical "starving author."

Whatever forces compelled Katherine Dalton Renoir to write fiction, between 1929 and 1951 the author as Moray Dalton published fifteen Inspector Hugh Collier mysteries and ten other crime novels (several of these with Hermann Glide). Some of the non-series novels daringly straddle genres. *The Black Death*, for example, somewhat bizarrely yet altogether compellingly merges the murder mystery with post-apocalyptic science fiction, whereas *Death at the Villa*, set in Italy during the Second World War, is a gripping wartime adventure thriller with crime and death. Taken together, the imaginative and ingenious Moray Dalton crime fiction, wherein death is not so much a game as a dark and compelling human drama, is one of the more significant bodies of work by a Golden Age mystery writer—though the author has, until now, been most regrettably overlooked by publishers, for decades remaining accessible almost solely to connoisseurs with deep pockets.

Even noted mystery genre authorities Jacques Barzun and Wendell Hertig Taylor managed to read only five books by Moray Dalton, all of which the pair thereupon listed in their massive critical compendium, *A Catalogue of Crime* (1972; revised and expanded 1989). Yet Barzun and Taylor were warm admirers of the author's writing, avowing for example, of the twelfth Hugh Collier mystery, *The Condamine Case* (under the impression that the author was a man): "[T]his is the author's 17th book, and [it is] remarkably fresh and unstereotyped [actually it was Dalton's 25th book, making it even more remarkable—C.E.]. . . . [H]ere is a neglected man, for his earlier work shows him to be a conscientious workman, with a flair for the unusual, and capable of clever touches."

Today in 2019, nine decades since the debut of the conscientious and clever Moray Dalton's Inspector Hugh Collier detective series, it is a great personal pleasure to announce that this criminally neglected woman is neglected no longer and to welcome her books back into light. Vintage crime fiction fans have a golden treat in store with the classic mysteries of Moray Dalton.

Moray Dalton's *The Body in the Road* (1930), *The Night of Fear* (1931) and *Death in the Cup* (1932)

In 1928 Agatha Christie, still disheartened and demoralized by a rapid succession of psychic hammer blows-- the recent death of her beloved mother, ongoing marital discord with her estranged husband Archie and her brief though highly publicized and embarrassing "disappearance" of two years earlier--published *The Mystery of the Blue Train*, her fifth Hercule Poirot detective novel and one the Queen of Crime remembered ever after with pronounced distaste. "Really, how that wretched book ever came to be written, I don't know!" she exclaimed with exasperation of *The Blue Train* in her posthumously published Autobiography, composed between 1950 and 1965. "I had no joy in writing, no élan," she recalled of those dismal days, adding bluntly:

> I had worked out the plot—a conventional plot, partly adapted from one of my other stories. I knew, as one might say, where I was going, but I could not see the scene in my mind's eye, and the people would not come alive. I was driven desperately on by the desire, indeed the necessity, to write another book and make some money.
>
> That was the moment when I changed from an amateur to a professional. I assumed the burden of a profession, which is to write even when you don't want to, don't much like what you are writing, and aren't writing particularly well. I have always hated *The Mystery of the Blue Train*, but I got it written,

and sent off to the publishers. It sold just as well as my last book had done.

Not only did the book sell well, but contemporary critical notices of the latest Hercule Poirot murder opus were good and modern mystery readers, obviously not burdened with Christie's emotional baggage, continue to give the novel good marks today. Moreover, whatever one's feelings about the quality of *The Mystery of the Blue Train*, there assuredly is found between its covers at least one notable character (aside from Poirot himself): a certain mysterious individual named Mr. Goby. Early in the novel this enigmatic private inquiry agent is consulted by American millionaire Rufus Van Aldin. (An inordinate number of American millionaires in Golden Age British mysteries seem to have come of Dutch extraction by way of New York, formerly New Netherland.) The demanding tycoon desires to collect dirt on his son-in-law, Derek Kettering, on behalf of his daughter, Ruth, who is planning, with her father's encouragement, to slap her errant husband with a divorce suit. In Chapter Five Mr. Goby is introduced to readers as "a small, elderly man, shabbily dressed, with eyes that looked carefully all around the room, and never at the person he was addressing." After concluding his succinct interview with Mr. Goby, who during the entire time successively gazes at the radiator, the left hand drawer of the desk, the cornice and the fender, but never at his client, a gratified Mr. Van Aldin confidently pronounces to his secretary: "That's a very useful man. . . . In his own line [the sale of information] he's a specialist. Give him twenty-four hours and he would lay the private life of the Archbishop of Canterbury bare for you." Despite his mild appearance, Mr. Goby, one imagines, could have gone toe-to-toe with Dashiell Hammett's private dick The Continental Op, who in novel form debuted the next year in *Red Harvest* (1929).

Despite her later dismissal of the worth of *The Blue Train*, Christie from some corner of her clever mind must have recollected Mr. Goby with gratification, for many years later she revived him in three additional Hercule Poirot mysteries: *After the Funeral* (1953), *Third Girl* (1966) and *Elephants Can Remember* (1972), the latter work the very last Poirot tale that she wrote. Elderly Mr. Goby ultimately enjoyed nearly as great longevity as the brilliant Belgian sleuth himself. Another crime writer upon whom Mr. Goby may have made an impression was Moray Dalton, whose sixth mystery novel, *The Body in the Road* (published in the UK and US in 1930, two years after *The Mystery of the Blue Train*), introduces a Mr. Glide, a Mr. Hermann Glide, who rather resembles Christie's own Mr. Goby. However, Mr. Glide in contrast with Mr. Goby is far from a minor character, being, rather, the man who actually solves the puzzling murders in *The Body in the Road* and two successor novels, *The Night of Fear* (1931) and *Death in the Cup* (1932).

In *The Body in the Road* Mr. Glide is first mentioned nearly four-fifths of the way into the novel. This is after Lord David Chant--formerly an investigator at Scotland Yard but now moodily ensconced at Spinacres, a rural estate in southern England, having against all odds inherited the family title--travels to London to meet with his former superior. Lord David is seeking advice on how to help the legally imperiled young woman whom he holds most dear: Linda Merle, a former piano accompanist in the town of Jessop's Bridge near Spinacres, who shockingly has been charged with the murder of her friend Violet Hunter, the beautiful, blonde and ingenuous violinist whom Linda Merle accompanied at the Tudor Café. Declaring that nothing can be done through official channels to help Lord David and his lady love, David's one-time Chief advises him to seek the aid of Hermann Glide. "I've heard of him," responds Lord David doubtfully of the private inquiry agent. "A bit of a mountebank, isn't he?" To which his Chief judiciously responds: "He is none too scrupulous about the means he employs to attain his ends, though I fancy he is clever enough to keep within the law. . . . we keep in touch with him here. We don't approve of him—but we find him useful."

Ushered into Mr. Glide's office by his loyal secretary, Miss Briggs, Lord David finds seated before him at a shabby desk a "little man, noticeably frail in appearance, with wistful brown eyes in a small puckered face," who rather reminds him of a "monkey on a barrel organ." Although, in contrast with Mr. Goby, Mr. Glide apparently can look his clients evenly in the face, he prefers to devote his surface attention to a lump of modeling wax, which during interviews he molds into "fantastic shapes" with his "long slender supple fingers." Yet Mr. Glide is paying close attention indeed to what Lord David has to tell him, and it is he who engineers a far happier outcome to the case than readers might well have expected when Glide was first consulted by the master of Spinacres, for things then looked very dark indeed for David and Linda. Just how Mr. Glide accomplishes this feat makes an ingenious finish to a most gripping tale of murder, which though primarily a detective novel shares some affinity with the

Golden Age thrillers of Edgar Wallace and Agatha Christie. (Over the course of the novel we observe two characters, both women, reading Edgar Wallace novels.)

A year after the publication of *The Body in the Road*, the perspicacious Mr. Glide reappeared, this time about forty percent of the way into the story, to solve another strange killing in *The Night of Fear*, Moray Dalton's bravura turn on a classic country house Christmas mystery. Family and friends and assorted servants were gathered at Laverne Peveril, home of George Tunbridge and his wife, when bloody murder struck, during what was meant to be a jolly holiday game of hide-and-seek. Evidence points to George's old public school friend Hugh Darrow, but this view is challenged by Inspector Collier, who made his first appearance a couple of years earlier in *One by One They Disappeared* (1929) and within a few years would supersede Hermann Glide as Moray Dalton's primary series sleuth.

The conscientious Scotland Yard inspector happens to be on the scene visiting his friend Sergeant Lane and at Lane's invitation he unofficially participates in the early stages of the investigation. He later briefly takes over the investigation after Lane is sidelined. However, at the behest of George's string-pulling cousin, Sir Eustace Tunbridge, Collier is pulled off the case and replaced by a disliked rival from the Yard, who proceeds to arrest Darrow. At Collier's suggestion, visiting American Ruth Clare, who loves Hugh dearly, turns to Hermann Glide for help—a most fortunate decision, as it transpires.

In 1932 Hermann Glide again arrives to save the day, this time in *Death in the Cup*, an absorbing account of murder in the poisoned bosom of a genteel, if alarmingly dysfunctional, family in Dennyford, a smugly insular provincial town in southern England that a visiting character ironically describes as a "peaceful little place . . . so typically English, almost Jane Austen still in the twentieth century, where the most exciting thing that could happen would be the lowering of somebody's golf handicap. . . ." Mr. Glide appears halfway through the novel, in service of Geoffrey Raynham (lately retired from the East), the concerned uncle of young Lucy Rivers, who is in love with Byronically handsome Mark Armour, the chief suspect of the local police in a most dreadful murder case. An offstage Inspector Collier acts as Glide's and Raynham's go-between.

As the title suggests, both the initial slaying (that of the unhappy Armour family's domineering and blindly unfeeling eldest sister, Bertha) and the one which follows it appear to have been accomplished by means of a poison classically favored by murderers in need: arsenic. Students of English true crime will recollect, as no doubt the author herself did, the unsolved poisonings at Birdhurst Rise, a Victorian villa in Croydon, south London. There between April 1928 and March 1929 a man, his sister-in-law and mother-in-law died most mysteriously, all of them in all likelihood from the ingestion of fatal amounts of arsenic. In contrast with the Croydon poisoning case, however, the killer in *Death in the Cup* is finally collared, with credit going once again to the wit and wiles of wizened Mr. Glide. Surely even Agatha Christie's Mr. Goby could not have put in a more impressive performance than Mr. Glide in these three superb Moray Dalton detective novels.

Curtis Evans

I
TROUBLE AT LAVERNE PEVERIL

"DEAD! Don't touch him, anybody, for God's sake! I—I'll ring up the police—"

Ten miles away Sergeant Lane of the Parminster constabulary stopped in the act of filling his pipe to look across at his friend. "That's the telephone. I'm off duty tonight, but if it's anything urgent they ring me up from the station, blast them! I hope I don't have to turn out a night like this."

He picked up the receiver. "Yes? . . . Is that you, Superintendent? Lane speaking. . . . Yes. . . . Very good. . . . May I take my friend along? . . . Yes, the one I brought round this morning. Unofficially, of course." He hung up the receiver and reached for his boots. "I've got to go, Collier. Some sort of trouble at Laverne Peveril. Mr. Tunbridge has just rung up the superintendent and I'm to go over at once. I thought, as you're keen, you might care to come along with me and give me the benefit of your experience—unofficially; the superintendent stressed that."

Hugh Collier smiled. "I know. You won't call in the yard until the scent is cold. Never mind, old chap. It's not your fault. There's not a grain of jealousy in your composition. I'll come like a shot."

"Right. The superintendent is sending round young Anderson with the car to pick us up. Here it is."

The two men put on their overcoats and clattered down the stairs, Lane stopping a moment on the way to tell his landlady not to sit up for him. The car was below. Lane took the driver's seat and Collier sat beside him while the young constable who accompanied them got in behind. It was freezing hard, and Lane, fearing a skid, drove carefully through the narrow winding streets of the little market town.

"Where is this place?"

"Laverne Peveril? Up the valley of the Clour. A ten-mile run. There is a shorter way, but the floods have been out since November and it's impassable." Neither spoke again until Lane was able to say, "There it is."

Collier looked at the long facade of the great house, glimmering white in the misty moonlight across the narrow valley, with open parkland in front and a background of woods. It was only a momentary glimpse before they turned in between two high gateposts surmounted with heraldic griffins and swept up a mile-long avenue of beeches to the front entrance.

The hall door was opened as they approached, and a burly figure appeared on the threshold, silhouetted against the light within, and waited for them to come up the steps.

"Are you the police?"

"I am Sergeant Lane."

"Have you brought a doctor?"

"Not with me. He's following on. He was out at a case when you rang up. Are you Mr. Tunbridge? What is the trouble?"

"Yes. Yes. Come in. Don't stand there in the cold."

Normally Mr. George Tunbridge was a bluff, hearty kind of person, with a loud, cheerful voice and a ready laugh, but he had obviously sustained a severe shock. His ruddy colour had faded to a mottled pallor and his hands shook. He was attired, rather oddly, considering that it was only just after ten o'clock, in a dressing-gown and pyjamas.

"The servants are all away at a dance at the village hall and they won't be back for another couple of hours at least," he explained. "They went off in the bus from the White Hart directly after dinner." Collier was looking about him. It was a large hall with several doors on either side and a staircase at the farther end. A pile of oak logs was burning on the open hearth of a cavernous fireplace which was partly screened by a three-fold panel of Spanish leather. There were deers' heads and antlers on the walls.

"Now, sir," Lane was saying, "if you'll just tell me in a few words what's wrong here we can be getting on with the job."

"Yes. To be sure. It's very painful. A terrible business." Tunbridge passed a trembling hand over hair that was beginning to grow thin. "We were playing hide and seek all over the house. In the dark, you know. I had switched off the light at the main. Two of us were seekers and the rest of the party hid. They were allowed twenty minutes, and at the end of that time we gave the signal with that gong over there and started looking for them."

"How would you do that in the dark, sir?"

"Oh, we each had an electric torch. Well, I'd just got to the first landing when I heard some one calling for lights down here. I came down and turned the light on at the main. The meter is just down the passage leading to the servants' quarters. Everybody had flocked into the hall by then. That is—with one exception, but I didn't realize that at the time. The person who had given the alarm, an old friend of mine, Hugh Darrow, was standing over there by the door that leads to what we call the long gallery. He was in white—I should explain that we'd all come down to dinner in fancy dress of sorts—and the sight of him gave us all the shock of our lives, for his sleeves and the front of his coat were smeared with blood. I—well—he said he'd found somebody dead in one of the window embrasures in the gallery. I told the women to remain in the hall, and my cousin, Sir Eustace Tunbridge, who is staying here, and I went to see for ourselves. We found the body of another of my guests, Edgar Stallard, the writer, lying on the window seat behind the curtains. There was—a lot of blood," added Tunbridge, with a shudder.

"I see." The country policeman glanced at the man from Scotland Yard and then back to the twitching face of the narrator. "Very upsetting," he said, sympathetically. "What did you do then?"

"We came back here, and I locked the gallery door, and then I rang up the police station at Parminster. We've been sitting in the library—the men of the party, that is. The ladies were very distressed, naturally, and I thought they had better go up to their rooms."

"Yes. Well, I think we'd better view the body first," said Lane. They followed Mr. Tunbridge across the hall to the gallery door. He unlocked it and moved aside to allow them to pass in.

"You won't want me, I hope," he said, apprehensively. Again Lane glanced at Collier, who replied with a slight negative motion of the head. Lane took his cue. "That's all right, sir. Wait for us in the hall, if you will. The doctor will be along any time now."

"One moment," said Collier, before they passed in. "Where does this gallery lead to?"

"To the annex. It was built out in my father's time for my mother, who was very musical. It's just a music-room.

There's an iron spiral staircase in it leading to the room above, which is reached by a passage over the gallery."

"I see. Thank you."

Left to themselves, Lane moved forward, while his companion stood for a moment to take note of the proportions of the gallery. He judged it to be about twelve feet in width by thirty in length. There were three windows on either side in deep embrasures covered with heavy curtains of rose-coloured velvet. The curtains of the middle window on the left were partly drawn. All the lights were on.

Collier joined his friend, and together they looked down at the inert sprawling figure of a man fantastically dressed in red-and-white-striped pyjama trousers, with a red sash belt and a white silk shirt open at the neck. A bandana handkerchief was bound about his head and he wore a black patch over one eye. The other glared up at them with what appeared to be blank surprise. There was, as Mr. Tunbridge had said, a great deal of blood.

"Did he kill himself?"

Collier shook his head. "Look at his hands gripping the edge of the window seat. He was taken unawares. And where's the weapon?"

Lane grunted. "Looks bad. I'll get a few measurements before the doctor comes." He had never had a murder case before but he had learned the routine. "Will you help me, Collier? I think Anderson had better remain where he is at the hall door, keeping an eye on things generally. I'll have to ring up headquarters. They'll have to send somebody along with a camera. I'd like a flashlight photo of the body before it's moved."

"No harm in having one," said Collier, "but don't put off your combing out of the house party too long. This house was plunged in darkness for rather more than twenty minutes, and during that time the crime was committed. There's a third door on the left apparently leading into the garden, but it's locked, and the key is here, on the inside. Mark that fact, Lane. It's important." He removed the key and sniffed at it before he replaced it. Then, going back to the window embrasure where Lane was already busy with a foot rule, he bent over the body.

"Aged about forty. Inclined to self-indulgence. Good-looking chap and quite aware of the fact. I dare say the poor devil fancied himself in that piratical get up, but a starched shirt front might have saved him by deflecting the blow. No sign of the weapon unless he's lying on it, and we'd better not move him before the doctor comes."

He stood up again, his shrewd eyes, very blue in his lean brown face, looking about him alertly. "I think I'll have a squint at the music-room."

The door at the far end of the gallery was closed but not locked. Collier, fumbling for the light switch, was conscious of a slight acceleration of his pulses. Had anyone thought of looking in here since the body was found? The murderer might be lurking near. But the light revealed an empty room. Collier's gaze travelled past the music cabinets and the cushioned divans, past the grand piano whose glittering black surface reflected his approach, to the spiral staircase.

II

IN THE DARK

THE DOCTOR had arrived and been left to carry out his examination of the body. Lane had spent ten minutes at the telephone. George Tunbridge, meanwhile, was talking volubly to Collier.

"Are you under the other, or what?"

Collier explained. "I'm attached to the Criminal Investigation Department at Scotland Yard, but I'm on holiday just now and spending a few days of it at Parminster with Lane, who is a personal friend of mine, though we haven't seen much of each other of late years. When this call came he obtained permission for me to accompany him unofficially. You understand, I've no authority. Sergeant Lane is in charge. If you object to my presence I shall have to retire, but I hope you won't for I confess I am interested."

"No, no, please stay!" cried Tunbridge. "Ah, here is the sergeant."

Lane joined them. "Now, Mr. Tunbridge, I shall have to trouble you for a list of the members of your house party. They'll all have to be interviewed, I'm afraid."

"Tomorrow morning will do for that, I suppose."

"I'm sorry, sir, but the matter is too serious to admit of delay. Now—" he produced his notebook. "Mr. Stallard was alive when the servants left for the village dance?"

"Most certainly. Manners, my butler, came into the dining-room to tell me they were just off. We heard the bus start before we all came out into the hall. Stallard passed out in front of me."

"We can count the servants out then. Yourself and Mrs. Tunbridge—"

"Well, there's my cousin, Sir Eustace Tunbridge, and his fiancée Miss Diana Storey, and her grandmother, Mrs. Storey. There's my friend Hugh Darrow, who found the—the body, and another old friend of mine, an American, Mrs. Clare. There's Angela Haviland, who is a kind of protégée of my wife's, and her brother Julian. Then Jack Norris came over from the vicarage with his sisters Barbara and little Joan, and two undergraduate friends of his. They were skating with us on the lake in the park earlier in the day."

"That's the lot? No one else?"

"No one."

"Fourteen in all. Well, I've got your statement, Mr. Tunbridge. I think I'll see Mr. Darrow first."

"I ought to tell you that Darrow is blind since the war, poor devil. I believe he's in the library with my cousin and young Haviland and the vicarage crowd. There's a little room here by the front door I use as a study. Shall I tell Darrow to come to you there?"

"That will do very well, Mr. Tunbridge."

When they were alone Lane turned to his companion. "He's very popular in the county, a good landlord and a generous subscriber to all the local charities. A real sport. I've never heard a word against him. Very easy-going. On the Bench he's all for letting offenders off and giving them another chance. What do you think of him?"

"He's very jumpy," said Collier, "but that's natural under the circumstances. Here comes number one on your list."

Lane sat down at the table as Hugh Darrow entered, and rose again to push forward a chair for him.

"Sit here, Mr. Darrow, if you please."

Hugh Darrow was thin and dark, with a mop of black hair brushed back from his forehead. His blue serge suit was very much worn and his slender beautifully shaped hands were noticeably ill-kept. He did not look either of the two policemen in the face but kept his large brown eyes fixed steadily on some point over their heads. Collier, who was a good judge of age, put him down as thirty-five.

"Now, Mr. Darrow, I'd like to have an account of your movements from the moment you all came into the hall after dinner. The time would be—"

"About a quarter to nine. We dined earlier tonight to give the servants time to dress for their dance. The others were laughing and talking. They all thought this game of hide and seek was going to be great fun. They were waiting to give Mrs. Storey time to get up to her room before the light was turned off at the main. She's quite an old lady, and naturally she didn't care to play. Well, the game started. There was a lot of giggling and screaming at first with everybody fumbling about in the dark. After about ten minutes it got fairly quiet and I guessed that the players had all dispersed to their hiding places. I had to make up my mind whether I'd go up to bed or join in the game. You see, I've been blind ever since I was blown out of a trench at Le Cateau thirteen years ago so that darkness is nothing new for me and not much fun. Still I decided I'd carry on, and I made for the gallery and slipped behind the curtains of the first alcove on the right as you go in."

Lane was scribbling busily. Collier was watching the blind man's face with a puzzled look on his own.

"The gong sounded pretty soon and I made sure one of the seekers would come into the gallery and find me, but neither of them did. Then, as I sat there I heard a steady dripping, like the ticking of a clock, but slower. It seemed to come from an alcove farther on. It was, I felt, rather horrible, but I was moved to investigate. I went over and reached round the curtain. I touched an arm, a shoulder, something warm, wet, sticky. Oh, my God! I—"

His voice, until then carefully under control, broke suddenly.

"All right, sir," said the good-natured Lane soothingly. "Take your time."

"That's all," he said, after a moment. "I rushed out into the hall and called for light. People came. Tunbridge and his cousin went in and found Stallard."

"Just so." Lane was drawing noughts and crosses on the blotter under his hand. "You know the way about the house pretty well, I suppose? You often stay here?"

"No. I spent my Easter holidays here once when I was about twelve. Tunbridge and I were at the same prep school. We met again during the war at a convalescent home for officers in Richmond and lost sight of one another afterwards. We met by chance a week ago in the Strand and Tunbridge asked me down here for Christmas. I arrived yesterday afternoon by the same train as the Havilands. I don't know anyone here except Mrs. Clare."

"You didn't know the dead man, Stallard?"

"No."

"I see. I am afraid you will have to stay on until after the inquest, Mr. Darrow. Your evidence will be required. Is your home in London?"

"Yes. I live in diggings at Turnham Green. I used to play the piano at a local cinema, but the music there is mechanized, and I have to depend on my basket work now and weaving."

"And your pension?"

"And my pension. Has this anything to do with the matter in hand?"

"Routine, Mr. Darrow. You mustn't mind. That's enough for the present. Thank you very much. Would you ask Sir Eustace to give me a few moments of his time?"

When he had left the room Lane appealed again to Collier. "Did you size him up?"

Collier shook his head. "I rather liked him," he said slowly, "but why is he so desperately unhappy? Of course he's highly strung. A mass of nerves. The artist type. But still—" He shrugged his shoulders. "We may get fresh light on his trouble from the others."

Sir Eustace Tunbridge proved to be a large pompous man, with a family likeness to his cousin George, but lacking his hearty good-nature.

"Here I am," he said as he sat down heavily, "and very glad to help you to the best of my ability, of course, with my advice and so forth. A most unpleasant affair. I hope for everybody's sake that it can be hushed up. I suppose there's no doubt that the wretched man committed suicide?"

"It wasn't suicide, Sir Eustace. We can rule that out."

"Good God! You don't say so! Then—have you discovered anything? An attempt to break in? Did he have a fight with a burglar? Though I can't imagine Stallard putting up much of a fight."

"Well, it's a possibility," said Lane cautiously, "though I've found no traces of a forcible entry and I shouldn't say there was any kind of struggle. No. He was taken by surprise. Did you know this Mr. Stallard well, Sir Eustace?"

"Certainly not. The fellow was a rank outsider. I couldn't stick him. Neither, I fancy, could my cousin. The women liked him. He was one of these writing chaps, you know. Not novels. Reminiscences and biography of the scandalous type and *réchauffés* of criminal trials. That sort of muck. He was gassing away only yesterday about a volume in preparation, a collection of murder mysteries from the nineties of the last century, little dreaming, poor devil, that he was destined to figure personally in anything of the kind. Have a cigar?"

"Thank you, sir. I'll keep it if I may to smoke later. I gather from what you say that he wasn't a general favourite with the gentlemen of the house party. Did he, to your knowledge, have an actual quarrel with anybody?"

"A quarrel? No." Sir Eustace's mental processes were slow. It was evident that he had not yet grasped all the implications. "A quarrel? Great Heavens! You're not suggesting that he was murdered by one of us?"

"I'm not suggesting anything," said Lane patiently, "but knives don't fall from the skies, you know."

"You have found the weapon?"

"Not yet. By the way, you took part in this game of hide and seek, Sir Eustace?"

"Well—yes, I did. I did not want to but I was over-persuaded. One does not like to be a spoilsport. When the lights were switched off I proceeded to the library and sat down in a comfortable chair. I didn't move when I heard the gong and only came out when the alarm was given."

"You were alone during that time?"

Sir Eustace frowned. Evidently this was a sore point. "I was alone. Is there anything else?"

"I think not, thank you. Would you be good enough to ask Mr. Haviland to come next?"

"Young Haviland? Certainly."

"Had a row with his young lady by the look of it," said Lane disrespectfully when the baronet had made his exit. "It's years since I played hide and seek but my recollection is that we hid in pairs."

Collier grinned. "Yes. Seems to have been a dullish game. Is he a widower? He must be past fifty."

"No. Everyone thought he was a confirmed old bachelor. His engagement was quite a surprise, I believe. He met the girl at Cannes this autumn. She's very beautiful, I hear, and not out of her teens. We don't seem to be making much progress, do we?"

"You've got to collect your evidence before you can sift it," said the Scotland Yard man. Both looked round as Julian Haviland entered.

Haviland was a slightly built graceful-looking young fellow. His eyelashes had been touched up with a blue pencil and his hair owed its tinge of gold to art. He was wearing a lavender silk dressing-gown over pyjamas of the same delicate shade.

The country bred Lane eyed him with ill-concealed disapproval but contrived to sound friendly. "This is a bad business, Mr. Haviland."

"Oh, putrid!" the young man agreed. "You don't mind if I smoke? Stout fellows!" He perched himself negligently on the arm of a chair. "Carry on with the Torquemada business."

Lane looked down at his notes. "I understand that you remained in the hall with Mr. Tunbridge when the rest of the party dispersed to find hiding places?"

"Yes. I was parked next to the gong, and I beat on it at twenty past nine."

"Was the darkness in the hall absolute?"

"Oh, rather! We'd put the Spanish screen round the fire. There was a glimmer of firelight reflected on the ceiling if you looked up. That was all."

"Mr. Darrow tells us that he lingered in the hall for about ten minutes before entering the gallery. Can you corroborate that?"

"My dear soul, haven't I just said that it was dark!"

Lane grunted. "How did you know it was time to sound the gong?"

"My wrist watch has a luminous dial."

"So you just sat and chatted with Mr. Tunbridge?" suggested Collier.

He had not spoken before.

"No. He was somewhere about but not near enough to talk."

Haviland shook the ash of his cigarette airily on to the carpet.

"Poor old George isn't frightfully keen on me, as a matter of fact. He thinks I'm wasting my lovely youth on trifles and all that. He'd like to push me out on to the great open spaces where men are MEN. It's Pearl—Mrs. Tunbridge, you know—who asked me and my sister down."

"I see," said Lane drily. "Is this your first visit?"

"Oh dear, no!"

"Can you throw any light on this tragedy, Mr. Haviland? Was Mr. Stallard on good terms with the other members of the house party? No quarrel or unpleasantness?"

The elegant Julian made a slight but expressive grimace. "The women thought no end of him. I must say I loathed him. I saw Sir Eustace looking very grim only yesterday when he was swarming round Diana Storey. Today he was trying to turn the head of little Joan Norris, one of the kids from the vicarage. But there hasn't been any row that I know of."

"Thank you. I think I'll see your sister next, Mr. Haviland, if you'll be good enough to ask her to come here. You can tell her we are not at all alarming."

"Oh, she'll enjoy herself. It'd take more than two policemen to rattle Angela," said her brother as he departed.

III
THE TORQUEMADA BUSINESS

COLLIER FOUND Angela Haviland more interesting than her brother. She was a scrawny, red-haired young woman, with a sharp little freckled face and the light lashes that are supposed to connote a tendency to double-dealing. Fancy dress, in her case, had been achieved by wearing a silk shirt and flannel slacks of Julian's. Her manner was assured, but Collier fancied that he detected some underlying anxiety.

"You want to know what I did when George turned off the light? I hid in the conservatory with Rags Norris and Bunny Brett. Rags knocked over a plant and Bunny broke a pane of glass. Just as well as things have turned out. It'll help us with our alibis. Oh, and we barged into Barbara Norris with Bertie Gunn."

"How do you get to the conservatory from the hall?"

"Through the drawing-room. There's another way in from the garden, of course, but we didn't go near that."

Lane brightened a little. He could write off six out of the fourteen, the vicarage party and this Miss Haviland.

"Who suggested hide and seek all over the house?"

She answered promptly. "I did. Pearl—Mrs. Tun-bridge—likes me to help her make things go. It was a change from bridge and dancing. I've played it often in other houses. It can be great fun. It's an opportunity for—well"—she shrugged her shoulders—"pairing off."

"You all remained in the conservatory until after the gong was sounded?"

"Until we heard somebody shouting."

Lane looked down his list of names. "What about the younger Miss Norris, Miss Joan?"

"She wasn't with us, but does it matter? I mean, I hope you'll leave her alone tonight. She's only seventeen, poor kid, and she's thoroughly frightened."

"I can't make any promises," said Lane. "What is she frightened about? Did she see or hear anything more than the rest of you?"

"I don't think so," said Angela. "It's just that—well—Stallard had been making the running with her all day, teaching her to skate and all that—and the little idiot was fancying herself in love with him. He went back to tea at the vicarage after spending the day on the lake and only came back here just in time to get into his pirate's rig-out for dinner."

Lane sat thoughtful for a moment, watching her shrewd little face. "Was Mr. Stallard a frequent visitor here?"

"He was never here before. The Tunbridges met him first last spring at Le Touquet. Pearl rather liked him. He dances well"—she corrected herself—"I mean—he danced."

"Can you think of anything, Miss Haviland, which would be likely to help us in our enquiry?"

"You mean suspicious-looking strangers lurking about in the village or the park?"

"Yes."

Lane had not meant that, but he preferred not to specify the kind of help he was hoping for. Collier intervened. "Was the house searched after the finding of the body?"

"I don't know. I don't think so. You see, it obviously wasn't a burglary. Nothing has been taken. I heard George say the door in the gallery that opens on to the north courtyard was locked and that the key was there on the inside."

Collier nodded. "Yes. We grasped the significance of that locked door, Miss Haviland. If the murderer left the house he would take that way. It was the nearest and the easiest. But the key turned on the inside involves the presence of a confederate under this roof."

"It's fairly obvious who did it, isn't it?" she said impatiently. "And I suppose he'll have to stand his trial, but he must have had some jolly good reason, and I should hope he'll be let off easily."

Both the detectives looked at her with startled faces. "You mean?"

"Well—Mr. Darrow. Naturally. He hated Stallard. I don't know why, but I heard him telling Mrs. Clare that he would never have come if he'd known Stallard would be here."

"I see," said Lane, after a pause. "That's very interesting. Then your theory is that the two men met in the gallery, that there was a quarrel, and that Darrow, in a moment of passion, stabbed the other and then rushed out to give the alarm?"

"It's the only possible explanation, isn't it?" she said. "He was the only person there. He came out, frightfully agitated, with his hands covered with blood."

"According to his own statement, Miss Haviland, he did not enter the gallery until ten minutes after the lights had been turned out. There would have been time for the murder to have been committed before he arrived on the scene if he is telling the truth."

"Oh, quite," she said.

Lane shook his fountain pen. "Thank you, Miss Haviland. That will be all tonight. I'd keep this idea of yours to yourself for the present, if I were you. I think I'll see Mrs. Tunbridge next if you'll be so good as to ask her to come in here."

"I'm awfully sorry, but I'm afraid you can't. At least—there'll be a fearful fuss if you insist. Pearl's very nervy and she was frightfully upset, of course. She broke down absolutely and George had to carry her upstairs. I helped her to bed and gave her a stiff dose of bromide. She'd be all muzzy if you talked to her now. She'll see you in the morning, of course. She'll be more anxious than anyone to help you, I know. Stallard was—was a great pal of hers."

"Very well," said Lane, "then we'll have Mrs. Clare in."

Angela got up briskly. "I'll tell her."

Ruth Clare did not keep them waiting. She was a woman in the early thirties. Evidently, like most Americans, she felt the penetrating chill of an English house with its inadequate heating, for she was wearing a fur coat over her dress of hydrangea blue chiffon. Her small pale face, lit by steadfast grey eyes, was set in lines of gravity, but Collier fancied that under happier circumstances those mobile lips might betray a quick sense of humour.

The sergeant was referring to his notes. "You are a native of the United States, Mrs. Clare."

"Yes. I was born in Virginia." Her soft drawling voice, with its caressing intonations acquired in childhood, was very attractive.

"You are an old friend of Mr. and Mrs. Tunbridge?"

"George Tunbridge was a patient at the hospital for wounded officers where I worked in nineteen-sixteen. I was over here with my mother when the war broke out and we couldn't get home because she was afraid of the submarines. I knew Mr. Darrow there, too."

"Do you often stay here?"

"No. This is my first visit. I met the Tunbridges in London and they asked me down for Christmas. I didn't know her before."

"Was Mr. Stallard another old friend?"

"He was not. Mr. Stallard was a complete stranger. I had read two or three of his books." Lane dropped his genial manner and made a sudden pounce.

"What cause had Darrow to dislike the dead man, Mrs. Clare?"

They both saw her flinch, but she answered steadily.

"You had better ask Hugh Darrow himself."

"I'm going to," said Lane grimly, "and meanwhile I must remind you that it is the duty of everyone here to assist me in this." He waited, but she said nothing.

"Very well," he said at last. "I'll pass on. Where did you hide and with whom during this game of hide and seek?"

She shivered a little, drawing her coat more closely about her. "I didn't really want to play, but Miss Haviland was so anxious that nobody should be left out. I was tired. We had been skating all day on the flooded meadows, and

I would much rather have gone to bed early. I just slipped back into the dining-room and round the screen that had been placed before the fire and knelt on the hearthrug trying to get warm. I only went into the hall when I heard Hugh's voice."

"You were alone all the time?"

"Yes."

"Thank you, Mrs. Clare. I won't trouble you any more tonight. You understand that everybody who was under this roof when the murder was committed will be expected to remain until after the inquest?"

"When will that be?"

"As soon as possible. It will be for the Chief Constable to decide. He will be coming over in the morning. Probably the day after tomorrow. Of course I don't know how long it will last."

"Thank you."

"I should like to see Miss Storey for a moment."

"She is in the hall with the others waiting to be questioned," said Ruth Clare. "Am I to tell her?"

"If you please."

She bowed slightly to both men and left the room. Lane looked at his friend. "What do you think of her?"

"She's all right," said Collier with conviction.

Lane rubbed his chin. "Oh, a very charming woman. But she didn't answer my question. You noticed that, of course?"

"And quite right, too," said Collier. "Darrow's an old friend. He's the kind of fellow women, nice women, are sorry for. I should have thought less of her if she'd given him away to the first bobby who came along nosing about for promotion."

Lane grinned back at him. "You're not in charge of the case, so you can afford to indulge in sentiment. I can't." He stopped as the door opened and Sir Eustace, rather fussily, ushered in his fiancée.

"There is no occasion for alarm, Diana. A matter of form. The sergeant will not keep you long. Sit here, my dear—"

Collier, standing back in the shadow, observed the ill-assorted couple curiously. Miss Storey did not appear to require reassurance. Her pink and white and golden prettiness, fragile and exquisite as blown glass, seemed quite untouched by the horror that had overshadowed the others. If she had been less lovely Collier might have thought she looked rather vacant. When she spoke her little tinkling voice accentuated her air of extreme youth.

"I don't mind. Only I'm awfully sleepy—"

Sir Eustace bent over her protectively. Lane, quite unconsciously, assumed a more deferential tone. Collier, looking on amused, did not know that his own face had softened. It was the tribute to which she had been accustomed all her short life and she took it as a matter of course. Men were nice to her, especially, perhaps, the older men.

"Where did you hide, Miss Storey?"

"Upstairs, in one of the unused bedrooms. I went to my own room first to get a handkerchief. I had meant to go down again but I heard people creeping about and I got rather nervous. It was very silly; but I am silly. So I just opened the door opposite my own and stood just inside until I heard Mr. Darrow calling for light."

"I see. Your grandmother, Mrs. Storey, had retired to rest before the game began?"

"Oh, yes. She thought it was silly. I don't know what she'll say when she hears about all this in the morning. She'll be dreadfully upset."

"I shall take you away in the morning," began Sir Eustace.

Lane intervened. "I'm sorry, sir, but I can't let anybody go until the inquest is opened. It's only a question of a couple of days. I won't trouble Miss Storey any further tonight—"

Diana Storey thanked him prettily and went out. Tunbridge lingered. "My cousin asked me to say that when the servants come back two rooms will be made ready for you."

"That's very kind of him," said Lane, "we shall be glad of a few hours' rest. Presently. We haven't finished yet."

"Really? It seems to me," said the baronet, and now that the girl had gone he had resumed his weightiest platform manner; "frankly, it seems to me that you are simply wasting time. These people came to commit a burglary and entered the house during dinner by way of the gallery. Unfortunately for himself Stallard discovered them hiding there and they killed him. They had a car, naturally, and by now they are miles away."

"We have found no traces of a forcible entry, Sir Eustace," said Lane, "but you may be right. We shall do our best." He was careful not to betray resentment if he felt any. Sir Eustace was a personage of considerable importance in the county.

IV
EXIT COLLIER

"HALLO!"

Collier woke to find the grey light of the December dawn in the room, and Lane, fully dressed, standing by his bedside.

"I'm going to have a look round outside," he explained. "There may be something in Sir Eustace's theory of a thief who made a getaway."

"I hope so for your sake," said Collier, yawning. "Pleasanter than having to fit a noose round the neck of one of the fourteen on your list."

Lane produced his pipe and filled it. He had had less than four hours' sleep and his face was lined with fatigue. He looked at his admired friend, the man who had got on, who was destined, he believed, for still greater things. "This sort of job is a bit beyond me," he confessed, "I feel the responsibility. I'm glad you're here with me, Collier."

"Rats!" said Collier vigorously. "You've started well, and you've got the chance of a lifetime with this case. Is the Chief Constable coming?"

"Yes. He'll be along any time after nine. He's a personal friend of the Tunbridges."

"Well, don't go asking for the assistance of the Yard. You may have to in a day or so, but I'd like you to pull this off yourself."

"Collier, I didn't ask you last night, but I must now. Have you any notion who committed this crime? Was it the blind man?"

"Darrow? I can't rule him out entirely," said the other slowly. "It was some one who knew the house well. Say that Stallard was stabbed some time between nine and ten minutes past when Darrow entered the gallery. The door into the courtyard was locked on the inside. The murderer must have escaped into the hall where Tunbridge and Haviland were waiting, or by way of the music-room and the spiral staircase to this floor. He may have hidden in one of the empty bedrooms and slipped out down the back stairs and out by the servants' quarters. There was a search of sorts before we arrived on the scene, but Tunbridge was too flustered to organize it properly."

"He says all the doors and windows were fastened. He tried every one himself," said Lane.

"He may have hidden somewhere until the servants came back and got away then. I don't say I think he did, but it's possible."

"The body will be removed to the coach house presently," said Lane. "I think I'll have another look at it first while you're dressing."

A quarter of an hour later, when Collier had just finished shaving, Lane burst into the room again.

"Collier, look at this!" He proffered a bloodstained scrap of paper. The pencilled writing on it was almost illegible but a few words could be deciphered.

. . . you without fail . . . nine . . .

"This is very interesting," said Collier. "Where did you find it?"

"In the dead man's left trousers pocket. There was nothing else but a handkerchief. He was in fancy dress, you remember, poor devil. He'd left his watch and note case and a heap of small change in a top drawer of his dressing-table."

"You've been through his room?"

"Not thoroughly yet."

"You'll have to find an opportunity to go through all the rooms some time," said Collier. "Well, this looks like an assignation. It may be nothing of the kind, but it's a fair assumption. Take care of this bit of paper, Lane."

"I'm going to. Would you say this crime was planned in advance, Collier?"

There was a discreet knock at the door. "Your breakfast is served in the study, sir."

The Chief Constable drove up in his car just as the two had finished their meal. He was a retired army officer, a tall thin man with a weather-beaten hatchet face and big bony hands covered with freckles and reddish hair. He greeted Lane and glanced at Collier. "Who's this?"

"A friend of mine, Colonel. He happened to be staying with me, and as he's in the C.I.D. at the Yard I was glad to have him along—" Lane, conscious of his superior's disapproval, faltered. "I thought there'd be no harm in him giving me the benefit of his greater experience."

"No doubt you meant well," said the Chief Constable stiffly, "but in my opinion it was an error of judgment. We can only judge your capacity by results, and this enquiry may give you a chance to prove your mettle. How can it if you have this—" He paused.

Collier supplied the name. "And may I say, sir," he added, "that I quite agree with you. I was interested, and glad to be with my friend, but I'd no thought of grabbing any of the bouquets that may be thrown. Would you like me to go now?"

Lane shot him an agonized glance, but Collier avoided meeting his eye.

"Candidly, I think it would be better," replied the Chief Constable. "If we think it necessary we shall apply to Scotland Yard for assistance in due course. Until then I should prefer to run my own show with my own men. Good morning." He turned to Lane, who by this time was scarlet with embarrassment. "Now I will hear your report."

Collier was too accustomed to local prejudices and jealousies to be much moved by this rebuff. He was sorry for his friend. Obviously the colonel was not an easy man to work with. He bowed to the Chief Constable, gripped Lane's hand hard with a cordial "Good luck to you, old chap," and walked out of the room. He little dreamed then how often he would recall that last glimpse of Lane's face, mutely protesting, as he closed the door. Ten minutes later he was walking down the avenue to the lodge gates on his way back to Parminster. A ten-mile tramp, but he was in the mood for it. The frozen grass crackled under his feet. Overhead the sky shone a clear pale blue through the network of bare boughs. On the left the ground sloped gradually down to the lake. Would some of the house party be skating there again today? After all, why not? They must pass the time somehow until the inquest was opened. He stopped when he had nearly reached the gates and looked back at the house. From that distance it was beautiful, shining like a pearl in the pale wintry sunshine against the russet and umber background of the leafless woods. Since last night a house with a secret. If walls could speak, what would they have to tell?

"Well—I'm out of it!" thought Collier as he struck the match for his cigarette and walked on, not without regret, for he hated to leave a riddle unsolved.

V
THE STOP GAP

COLLIER WAS sitting over a late breakfast the following morning when his friend's landlady came in to ask him to answer the telephone. He took up the receiver, expecting to hear Lane's voice.

"Hallo? Is that you, Lane?"

"No. I am Superintendent Inskip. Will you come round at once?" The police station was only a stone's throw away. Collier was shown into the Superintendent's room within five minutes. He found the Chief Constable there with Inskip. Both men looked worried. Colonel Larcombe held out his hand.

"I hope you didn't mind my shooing you off yesterday, Inspector?"

"Not in the least," said Collier, wondering what was coming next.

"The fact is we're in a hole. Lane is a casualty. Oh, nothing serious, I trust, but some one will have to take his place, and several of our best men are down with flu. Another point is that my personal relations with George and Eustace Tunbridge make things a bit awkward all round. So that—in short—I've decided, with the concurrence of Inskip, to call in the Yard after all, and we thought that as you were on the spot you might take over at once."

"You'll have to get into touch with headquarters, sir, about that. I'm quite willing, but I'm on holiday."

"Yes, yes. Quite. I'll arrange all that if you'll carry on."

"What has happened to Lane, sir?"

The Superintendent answered. "He was staying over-night at Laverne Peveril as Mr. Tunbridge kindly offered to put him up. The butler rang us up an hour ago. Lane had asked to be called early. The housemaid who went to rouse him found him unconscious and the room full of gas. The doctor's gone with the ambulance to fetch him."

"Is it—serious? He's an old friend of mine."

"I hope not," said the Superintendent. "You'll find Anderson there and he has been instructed to hold over Lane's notebook. He was to have made his report to me this morning."

"Has anything been settled regarding the inquest?"

"Yes. It's difficult at this season. The coroner has arranged to hold it in the village schoolroom tomorrow morning at eleven. He need only take formal evidence of identification and adjourn. The post mortem will be over and the funeral can take place. No relatives have come forward, and I understand that Mr. Tunbridge is seeing to everything."

Collier nodded. "Can I have the loan of a car? A motorcycle would do."

"Of course."

The police ambulance was just emerging from the lodge gates as Collier, who had covered the ten miles in record time, slowed down to take the curve. He put on the brakes and signalled to the driver to stop while he jumped out to speak to the doctor.

"How is Sergeant Lane?"

"You were here with him the other night?"

"Yes. I belong to Scotland Yard. I'm taking charge. How is he?"

"I hope we may pull him round. It's carbon monoxide poisoning, you know. I'm taking him to the hospital. Are you an old friend of his?"

"Yes."

"Do you know if he walked in his sleep?"

"I never heard of it. Why?"

The doctor lowered his voice. "It might account for the fact that the gas fire in his room was turned full on but unlit."

Collier's face changed slightly. "It might, as you say. I thought it was an escape. Thank you, doctor. Shall I be able to get a bed in the village?"

The doctor's smile was grim. "Taking no chances? Wise man. Yes. The White Hart. I shall be doing the post mortem on Stallard this afternoon. Shall you want to hear the result?"

"Yes."

The ambulance passed on, leaving a faint reek of disinfectants on the icy air. Collier, who had come from Parminster at sixty miles an hour, drove very slowly up the avenue to the house. Anderson, the young constable who had accompanied him and Lane on the night of the murder, was waiting for him at the foot of the steps.

"Good morning, Anderson."

"Good morning, Inspector. I have Sergeant Lane's notebook here to hand over according to instructions received by phone. It was on the dressing-table with his watch and fourteen shillings and ninepence in silver and coppers, and a penknife, a hank of string and a potato."

Collier stared. "A potato?"

"The Sergeant was inclined to rheumatism," explained Anderson. "There's a good many think a potato's a help."

"I see," Collier said. He had forgotten for the moment that Lane was country bred. He was smiling as he took the notebook and turned over the leaves. Rather abruptly his smile faded. He looked closely at the book for a moment and then closed it and slipped it into his pocket without comment.

"Now, Anderson, can you tell me what the sergeant did yesterday?"

"Well, he said to me, 'We must look for the weapon,' and we had a good hunt for it but we didn't find it. And he spent some time in the murdered man's bedroom, and some time after that in the library, and he talked to some of the servants, especially to Miss Berry, the first housemaid."

"He didn't tell you how he was getting on?"

"No, but he seemed pleased, and if you ask me, Inspector, I should say he was on the track of something."

"I see. Thank you, Anderson. I wish you'd put a rug over the radiator of my car—"

There was nobody in the hall when Collier passed through. He went upstairs to the room down the passage to the left that had been hastily made ready for Lane when the servants had returned from the dance in the village on the night of the murder. He found a middle-aged woman in a pink print dress and white cap and apron stripping the sheets from the bed.

"Are you Miss Berry?"

"Yes."

"You discovered the escape of gas here?"

"Yes."

The servants were, of course, inimical, resenting the presence of the police in the house. It was his business to break down their prejudice and make them talk. He asked some further questions, and from her brief and grudging answers learned that Lane had been in bed when she entered, and that he was wearing the pyjamas lent him by the butler, while his clothes were neatly folded on a chair.

"Can you account for the gas having been turned on, Miss Berry?"

"I think the leg of this chair pushed against the tap. You see—like this—and that he switched off the light and got into bed without noticing."

"I see." Collier pushed the chair back and stooped to the tap.

"Yes, I've done it now." He looked quickly round the room. "Have you cleared up at all here? I mean the waste paper basket and any odds and ends?"

"Not yet. There hasn't been time. But there isn't anything."

"I noticed that. About Mr. Stallard's room. You haven't touched that?"

"No. Sergeant Lane said we were to leave it and he took away the key. But, of course," she added acidly, "any one of the other door keys would have fitted."

"Will you come with me to his room now?"

"I've got my work to do—" she began.

He whirled round on her. "Good God, woman! A capital crime has been committed in this house: Murder! And you stand there—"

She shrank from him, startled at last out of her complacency.

"I—oh, you did give me a turn! What can I do?"

"Come with me and answer my questions." Stallard's room was as he had left it when he went down to dinner the night of his death. He was the kind of man who makes liberal use of toilet creams and powders, and on that evening he had had the excuse of fancy dress. The toilet table was covered with an array of little jar and bottles. Collier went systematically through them all, unscrewing the lids and sniffing the contents. Then he opened the drawers and looked into the wardrobe. "Silk underwear, and plenty of it." A portable typewriter in its case stood on the table. Collier looked at it and pulled out the table drawer. There was nothing in it but a few unused sheets of quarto and a crumpled purple carbon. He stood for a moment looking down at them thoughtfully.

"Did he do much work here, Miss Berry?"

"I've often heard him tap-tapping away, and Miss Haviland complained that he kept her awake in the next room."

"I wonder what he did with his stuff," mused Collier.

"Isn't there anything of what he wrote in the drawer?"

"Neither in the drawer nor in the waste paper basket. And gas fires in both rooms. You can't burn much in a gas fire without leaving tinder about. Besides—why burn? Very interesting, this absence of the written word. Two negatives make an affirmative. I learnt that at school—"

"I don't know what you're talking about," said Miss Berry, but she had lost much of her primness. He had succeeded in rousing her interest. "But it's queer there should be nothing in this table drawer. He did a lot of writing and scribbling. I've seen him at it when I've been in with his hot water."

"You did this room yourself?"

The head housemaid drew herself up. "It should have been one of the underhousemaids—but Millie came to me half crying one morning to complain of something Mr. Stallard had said to her. She's a good girl as I know, for she's my own sister's child, and I told her I would take her place until he went."

Collier nodded. He had already gathered a good deal of information regarding the manners and morals of the deceased. He thanked Miss Berry and let her go after warning her not to repeat their conversation.

Stallard had used his typewriter every evening, but had left no typescript. That was one queer thing. The other—

Collier slipped Lane's notebook from its elastic band and examined it. Hadn't he seen the dear old chap, his broad red face puckered with the mental effort required, jotting down his laborious accumulation of facts and impressions before he lay down to rest on the night of the murder? They were all here. But why had he made no further entries? Or—had he—? It seemed to Collier that several pages had been torn out.

VI
DOWN THE VALLEY

ONLY A FEW of the house party came down to breakfast in the big dining-room. The three young men from the vicarage consumed bacon and eggs and sausages with a hearty appetite and their efforts to maintain the decent gravity required by the occasion were only partially successful. Barbara Norris was upstairs looking after her little sister Joan who, in addition to considering herself heartbroken, had developed an influenza cold. Julian Haviland was an habitually late riser and seldom appeared until everyone had finished. Angela was pouring out the tea and trying to reassure George Tunbridge. "There's no need to get all hot and bothered about Pearl, really! She's had a shock, and you know how highly strung she is."

Sir Eustace was holding forth to a rather pale and silent listener. "I shall be taking Mrs. and Miss Storey back to Town in my car presently, Mrs. Clare, and I should be very pleased to give you a lift. We are only in the way here, and I hardly think we shall be required by the police to give evidence at the inquest. It is very unfortunate that we should be mixed up in such an unsavoury business, though I haven't said much to poor George to harass him further. It will be a lesson to him to be more careful in future about whom he asks down here."

"I'm afraid I don't understand," said Ruth Clare coldly.

"Well, you must see that he had introduced two unknown quantities." He lowered his voice to a confidential whisper, turning in his chair so that his broad back screened her from the others at the long table. "De mortuis—we know all that—but the fact remains that the dead man was a complete outsider. Mrs. George picked him up God knows where. This damned dancing craze. She gets her own way. Handsome woman, but a devil of a temper, and my poor cousin will do anything for a quiet life. And this fellow Darrow—"

Ruth interrupted. "Mr. Darrow is all right. He's an old friend of your cousin's—and of mine."

Sir Eustace's conversational methods were those of the steamroller. He proceeded weightily. "George and Darrow were at the same preparatory school, but we knew nothing of his people. They met again during the war when they were together at Richmond. Afterwards George lost sight of him completely and only came across him by chance last week in the Strand. I understand that he was overheard telling somebody that he wouldn't have come to Laverne Peveril if he had known Stallard would be here—"

Ruth set down her coffee-cup. Her hands were trembling. She had meant to keep out of this, not to take sides, but how could she refrain with that rather shabby figure of the blind man, seated a little apart from the others, before her eyes. She looked towards him as she spoke. "You can't possibly suspect him, Sir Eustace."

"Not of the actual stabbing—though you have to remember that that was done in the dark. By Jove, now I come to think of it"—Sir Eustace became animated—"the darkness that handicapped us would not affect him. However, it's more likely that he admitted an accomplice from outside and let him out again before he gave the alarm. That would account for the fact that the weapon has not been found. I must suggest that to the detective who has come to take Lane's place. Rather a pity they've had to swap horses while crossing the stream, but it's a mercy it was no worse. Nasty accident. I don't like gas fires in bedrooms myself."

Ruth pushed back her chair. She felt that if she remained there any longer she might be led into saying something that she would regret later. Darrow had just left the dining-room. She found him standing, evidently uncertain what to do next, at the foot of the stairs. She had meant to take the more prudent course and pass by, but something forlorn in his attitude touched her heart, and she stopped impulsively.

"Hugh—"

The haggard face brightened perceptibly as it turned towards her.

"Hugh, I'm going down to skate on the lake again. Won't you come with me? You can skate, can't you?"

"Yes. But—you haven't forgotten? You'd have to hold my hands—"

"Well, I could bear to do that." She hurried on, with a sudden sense that silence might be dangerous. "I'll get my fur coat and cap and join you. I'll get the skates too. George showed me where they were kept—"

Neither spoke much on the way down to the lake. Mist hung about the valley. It was a still morning, bitterly cold, and the frozen grass crackled under their feet as they left the avenue and went down the steep slope to the water's edge. The Havilands were there already with young Norris and his friends. Ruth steered her companion to a point a hundred yards farther along.

"I'll put on your skates," he said.

"Can you?"

"Of course."

He knelt at her feet to do it, his dark head bent, his thin brown fingers busy with the straps. She stood by while he adjusted his own.

"Now! It's all clear in front. The flood water was out over the meadows. We needn't stay on the lake. George said it would be safe if we kept well to the right away from the stream—"

They took hands and swept out together. Rags Norris, picking himself up after a fall, looked after them. "I say! Those two can skate! Doesn't Mrs. Clare look ripping in her furs!"

"Some furs!" said Angela critically. "That coat cost three hundred pounds if it cost a penny. Queen Cophetua and the beggarman. But of course she's only amusing herself."

They had left the tree encircled pool and were a mile farther down the flooded valley when Ruth said, "We'll stop now."

For a minute after they had come to a stand Darrow kept her gloved hands firmly clasped in his, feeling their warmth strike through to his starved heart. A great silence surrounded them, a silence broken only by their own quick breathing and, after a while, by the faint desolate chirping of some half-frozen bird. It seemed that they were the only living creatures under that iron sky. It was strange, thought Ruth, that in so death-like a setting she should be conscious of a physical well-being and a mental exhilaration such as she had not felt since she was a girl in her teens. Darrow's grip on her hands tightened. "Do you remember Richmond Park—the last day of my leave?"

"Yes." She sighed. "But that was in spring. Fourteen years, Hugh. That poor bird! Do you hear it? I wish I had thought to bring some crumbs."

She looked pityingly at the tiny rumpled robin that sat shivering on a branch of a half-submerged willow.

"I've got the sandwiches you asked for," he reminded her.

"How silly of me! Of course. That's fine. There's a bit of higher ground above the flood level just here, with the remains of an old hay rick. We can sit down and have our lunch. Give me your hand again and I'll guide you. There—"

He pulled out some of the hay for her and they sat down together to share the sandwiches and a thermos flask of coffee. After a while the robin flew down and hopped about their feet picking up the crumbs Ruth threw to him. They were both rather silent again, the keen edge of their brief ecstasy blunted.

He spoke after a while. "You are a widow?"

"Yes. Wilbur died."

"You are not in mourning?"

"No. It's over a year since. Besides—we were separated before that. It—it wasn't a happy marriage."

"I'm sorry," he said, but his heart leapt at her tone. He had to remind himself of what her mother had said to him on that last day at Richmond. "Please don't speak to Ruth about your feeling for her. She's so young. I don't want her to be tied. She likes you, but—forgive me—you are poor. My little girl needs the setting that only a rich man can give her."

She had had her way with them both, for he had returned to France without speaking, and had dropped out of their lives, while Ruth, going back to the States with her mother after the Armistice, had married soon afterwards a man of whom her family approved. He did not need eyes to tell him that she had the delicate precise finish, the patina that is only acquired by a woman who has both means and leisure. He recalled the worn patch on the sole of his shoe that he had discovered while fitting on his skates and the threadbare state of the overcoat which would have to last out this, its third winter. He smiled grimly at his own folly.

Ruth, watching his face, which was more expressive than he knew, rose to her feet. "We ought to be getting back. We shall get chilled here, and it looks like snow." She guided him on to the ice and they joined hands again. On and on with a rhythmic sweep that brought with it a sense of illimitable power, of an effortless swooping forward, like the strong-winged flight of a bird, to the end of the world and over the edge into space. An illusion. They had made too wide a curve bringing them too near the course of the stream flowing through the valley, and the ice cracked ominously. Ruth saw the jagged line appear at their feet and wavered for an instant, but Darrow urged her on.

"Faster! Faster! Bear to the left—"

They skated on, leaning forward, straining nerve and sinew, with that sound in their ears to spur them.

"I can't," she gasped presently. "I must rest. It's all right now." They had reached the lake. It was deserted. The others, warned by the gathering darkness of an impending storm, had gone back to the house. Silently Darrow removed his companion's skates and his own.

"We were nearly through," she said.

"Yes."

She laid a hand on his arm to guide him. "It's been lovely," she said, almost timidly. And then, after a pause: "Sir Eustace is planning to get Mrs. Storey and Diana away before the inquest. He seemed to think he could fix it with the Chief Constable. He offered me a lift back to Town in his car."

"Good!" said Darrow. "I hate to think of your being involved, however remotely, in this beastly business."

"Couldn't you get away too, Hugh?"

He laughed shortly. "Quite impossible. I'm a star turn. I found him, unfortunately for myself. Do you remember my telling you that I loathed the beast?"

"Yes—"

"Some one—that red-haired girl, Miss Haviland—overheard and passed it on to the police. Sergeant Lane was interested. I'm sorry he's a casualty, though. He was a decent chap."

"His friend from Scotland Yard is nice, too," said Ruth, but in a far-away voice, as if her thoughts were elsewhere. How did he know that Angela's hair was red? She cast a puzzled unhappy glance at her companion and increased her pace as if anxious to get back to the house. He was quick to feel that she was no longer at her ease with him, but he made no attempt to mend matters. He did not speak again until they reached the pillared portico over the front door. They could hear the voices of their fellow guests in the hall.

"This is the end," he thought. Aloud he only said, "Thank you, Ruth."

She passed in before him without answering. She was very pale.

VII
A GLIMPSE BELOW STAIRS

COLLIER OPENED the door that led from the first floor corridor running the length of the house to the back staircase, and listened to a burst of French like the pattering of small shot. He had worked hard at his French but he could only distinguish a word here and there. The speaker was a woman and, obviously, an angry woman. When she ceased there was a momentary silence, and then the sound of a man's footsteps retreating.

Collier grinned to himself. "She's got her knife into somebody." Her knife? But the servants had a collective alibi. They were all at the village hall when the murder was committed. He recalled what he had heard of Justine Dubois, Mrs. Tunbridge's French maid, and her unpopularity with her fellow servants. He had reached the landing and was looking over the banisters when the baize-covered door of the passage leading to the servants' quarters was pushed open and Sir Eustace's chauffeur came into the hall. Collier had noticed him in the stable yard when he arrived, cleaning his employer's car. He was a good-looking young man and the smart dark green uniform and black leggings became him very well. He stood, waiting, after a glance at the clock. Evidently it was his habit to come for orders at a certain hour.

Sir Eustace emerged from the library, carrying the *Times* and smoking a cigar.

"Good morning, Ivan. Is she all right? I thought there was a slight creaking yesterday."

"I have attended to that, Sir Eustace."

"Good. I think we shall go back to Town today. Ah— here is Mrs. Storey. Would you be ready to start immediately after lunch, Mrs. Storey?"

Mrs. Storey had been in her youth a very beautiful woman. At seventy she had preserved an air of distinction and remained an imposing figure, erect and dignified, with her silvery white hair and her black lace shawl fastened at the throat with a cameo brooch. She had devoted herself since her granddaughter left school to finding a gilded frame for her, and the capture of Sir Eustace Tunbridge, whom they had met that autumn in Cannes, was a proof of her skill and pertinacity, for the girl herself had been passive, and had done nothing but look lovely and answer in monosyllables the remarks addressed to her. "You see what she is—young and malleable," the old lady had said indulgently to the suitor. With Diana she was more downright. "You're a fool, my dear, but lots of men prefer that.

He's rather old for you, but we can't afford to wait. We're living beyond our means. I got all these frocks for you on credit—"

"Good morning, Ivan. I hope your toothache is better?" Mrs. Storey was always very affable with servants. Her tips when she gave any were small. She cherished the illusion that if she discussed the weather and enquired after their ailments and their relations a shilling would do as well as half a crown.

The young chauffeur saluted and answered respectfully. "Thank you, madame. It is gone."

"If I had known of it I would have given you some aspirin."

"Thank you, madame. The cook gave me aspirin."

"Oh—the cook—"

"Well, what about it?" said Sir Eustace rather testily. "Can you be ready by—say—two o'clock? Where is Diana?"

The girl had come out of the drawing-room in the wake of her grandmother. Sir Eustace's heavy middle-aged face brightened at the sight of her and he laid a big red hand possessively on her slender shoulder.

"Run up and pack your fallals. After all, Christmas in Town can be pleasant. A week at the Savoy as my guests before you go back to your rooms at Earl's Court."

She looked enquiringly at her grandmother, like a child. The old lady nodded. "Of course. Delightful. It's very kind of Sir Eustace. Come along, darling. We must get our things together."

They came upstairs, Collier stepping back to allow them to pass. Sir Eustace went back to the library and the chauffeur left the hall by the way he had entered.

The Inspector waited until the coast was clear before he descended. He needed a little time for consideration before he tackled Sir Eustace or Sir Eustace tackled him. Lane had said very distinctly that he expected everyone who had been in the house at the time that the murder was committed to remain at Laverne Peveril until the inquest had been opened, and the Norrises, keeping to the letter of the bond, had remained, though the vicarage was close to the park gates. Collier did not see why he should make an exception in favour of Sir Eustace and the Storeys though they had no evidence to give bearing on the tragedy and were not likely to be called as witnesses. The old lady, who had gone up to her room before the game of hide and seek began, had slept through it all and there seemed no reason to doubt that Diana Storey and her elderly fiancé had given an accurate account of their movements.

Collier, who had retreated to the little room called the study that had been used by Lane, lit a cigarette and threw the match into the fire. The local authorities would be anxious to oblige a county magnate who was a big landowner and a generous subscriber to various funds, but what would they say at the Yard? Perhaps there, too, a man like Sir Eustace might have influence. Collier shrugged his shoulders. "I suppose I had better let him go," he thought, and turned as some one rattled the doorhandle. "Come in."

His visitor, the first to come unasked, was Mrs. Tunbridge's maid, a fat young woman with a slack red mouth and angry eyes.

"I wish to speak to you—"

Collier noted that her English was excellent. Yet she had been raving in her own language a few minutes earlier. To whom? He indicated a chair. "Please sit down, mademoiselle."

He seated himself at the desk. "You have some information for the police?"

"I 'ave." Like many foreigners she had difficulty with her aspirates, especially when she was excited. "You 'ave not troubled yourselves about the servants. They have an alibi, no? All dancing—" She paused, apparently for dramatic effect.

Collier smiled at her. "Well, they were, weren't they?"

She drew a long breath. "All but one. All but one!"

The Inspector stiffened to attention, but his tone was still colloquial. "How was that?"

"The Russian. Ivan Pavlovski. The chauffeur of Sir Eustace. At the last moment he said he had toothache and he would not come. He went to bed. Maybe! Who is to prove it? He has a room over the garage, away from the house. When we came home after midnight all was confusion. No one thought of 'im. No one saw 'im until the next morning."

"Oh!" That just showed, thought Collier, what came of taking anything for granted. Of course there might be nothing in it. Mademoiselle Dubois was evidently out to make mischief. He eyed her thoughtfully and with no great liking. "Thank you for telling me. I'll see what he has to say about it. How is Mrs. Tunbridge, by the way? I'd like to have a few words with her sometime today."

"Is it necessary? She is very nervous, *très souffrante, pauvre dame*. The other agent saw her yesterday afternoon."

"I'm afraid I shall have to ask her to grant me a short interview," said Collier. He rose to indicate that the audience was at an end and opened the door for her to pass out. When she had gone he went to find Sir Eustace in the library. He was there with his cousin.

"Excuse me, Sir Eustace, but how long have you had your chauffeur? I should like all the particulars you can give me."

"What for? He's a decent young fellow. None of the servants were about—"

George Tunbridge joined in. "For Heaven's sake, Inspector, don't go upsetting the servants. We don't want to add a domestic crisis to our other troubles."

"I'm sorry, sir, but it's come to my knowledge that the chauffeur—not your man, Hodgetts, but the visitor—didn't go to the dance on the night of the murder. He complained of toothache and went to bed early—or so he says."

"If he said so you can take it from me that it is so," said Sir Eustace testily. "He's a most reliable man."

"How long has he been in your employment, Sir Eustace?" Collier persisted.

"Let me see. I engaged him last spring in Paris. He was with me there for a time and went with me down to the Riviera."

"He had good references?"

"Excellent. He had been two years with a French baroness. Really, Inspector, isn't all this rather a waste of time?"

Collier answered quietly. "That is for me to decide, sir. I shall have to ask him a few questions."

"Oh, all right. If you must you must," said Sir Eustace gruffly.

"And I'm afraid that as his alibi depends only on his own statement he will have to remain here until the inquest has been opened."

"But I want him to drive me up to Town this afternoon!"

"I'm sorry."

The baronet was used to having his own way. George Tunbridge, fearing an explosion, glanced deprecatingly from one to the other. "My dear chap," he said, "of course the Inspector has to do his duty and all that. I'd be awfully glad if you'd stay. Diana's a charming girl and the old lady one of the best bridge players I've ever come across. I know this terrible business has spoilt your visit here and that kind of thing, but I do wish you'd stick to the ship a bit longer, what? But if you'd rather not I can lend my fellow Hodgetts to push the old bus along, and Ivan can join you in Town when the police have done with him."

"Thank you," said his cousin coldly.

Collier retired, in good order but with a rather flushed face, to ring the study bell and ask the butler that the Russian chauffeur might be sent up to him. Pavlovski came promptly and answered every question put to him without any sign of reluctance and with an air of candour that impressed Collier very favourably.

It was quite true that he had not been to the dance with the others. He had a raging toothache and had retired to bed with various remedies pressed upon him by sympathizers. The cook had given him aspirin and Miss Berry some decoction of herbs brewed by herself. The parlourmaid had contributed menthol.

Obviously his youth and good looks had had their effect with the women. "And Mrs. Tunbridge's maid—Mademoiselle Justine?" hinted Collier.

For the first time Pavlovski hesitated, betraying a desire to evade the point. "She—she thought I ought to go all the same. She wanted me for her partner. The others only know easy dances. I explained that my tooth hurt me too much, but she was angry."

"Which tooth is it?"

"Up here, at the back."

"You went up to your room over the garage, took some of the stuff that had been given you, and slept round the clock?"

"That is so. I heard nothing at all. In the morning only I knew what had happened from the others."

"You speak English fluently. Have you been much in England?"

"Never before I came over last month with Sir Eustace."

"How did you learn the language?" asked Collier, surprised.

There was a perceptible pause. Then the young Russian answered very quietly. "When I was a child I had an English nurse. My parents were rich. We had a big house on the Nevski Prospect and many servants. That was before the revolution. Now everybody is dead. All who did not run away. And the house is burned. May I go now? I have to make sure that there is enough petrol for the journey—"

"I see. Yes, you can go now. But you will have to stay here until the inquest is opened. I have informed Sir Eustace."

"Is he angry?"

Collier's official severity relaxed somewhat. "He's not overpleased. Mr. Tunbridge has offered his chauffeur in your stead."

"They will go up without me?" said the young man, with a lost look.

Collier reassured him. "It'll be all right. You can join him in a day or two. He's annoyed, but not with you. He thinks very highly of you."

His well-meant words did nothing to lighten the Russian's gloom. He drew himself up, saluted, and left the room in silence. Collier remained for a moment in thought. He was not disposed to attach much importance to what he had just heard. Justine Dubois's motive in trying to make trouble for the young Russian was obvious. She had been trying to vamp him without success. A dangerous woman of the type that will go to any length to avenge wounded vanity. She might have killed Stallard—

Manners was cleaning his silver when the detective walked into the pantry.

"So Pavlovski didn't go to the village with the rest of you the night before last?"

"No. The poor lad had the face-ache." The old butler took up a soup ladle and polished it diligently. "At least— between you and me, Inspector, it wasn't that so much as that he didn't care to be tied up with ma'amzelle the whole evening. She'd wormed it out of him that he could dance the tango and all those fancy steps. She's made his life a burden ever since he came. He's one of the quiet reserved sort and only wants to be left alone."

"I thought as much," said Collier. "She went all the same and danced every dance, I suppose?"

"She did, she certainly did," agreed the butler, with a reminiscent chuckle; "wearing one of those dresses without a back, held up by tack, as they say. You should have heard what the cook thought—"

Collier went back to the hall. He could hear one of the Tunbridges in the library telephoning. What next? If he only knew what Lane had been doing the previous day! Those three pages torn from his notebook might make all the difference. He looked at his watch. Ten minutes to one.

He would have to wait until after lunch to see Mrs. Tunbridge and Joan Norris. He knocked at the library door and was told to come in. Sir Eustace, who was alone, was just hanging up the receiver. He went out without speaking to Collier. The Inspector glanced about him appreciatively. The library was lit by four French windows opening on the terrace. The walls were lined with books. A portrait of George Tunbridge's mother by Millais with George himself, a toddler in a white muslin frock and a blue sash, clinging to her skirts, hung over the Adam mantelpiece. A huge fire of oak logs burned on the hearth. The smell of wood smoke was mingled with that of leather bindings and tobacco. The atmosphere of such a room was one of peaceful security. Collier sighed. It was his fate never to enter such houses as these under normal conditions. He took up the receiver and asked for the Parminster cottage hospital. After a while he was put through to the secretary's office. He learned that Lane had been given a private ward. He had not yet recovered consciousness.

VIII
SPADE WORK

WHEN GEORGE TUNBRIDGE married her, during his last leave before the Armistice, Pearl was a member of a touring concert party. Though she had complained bitterly of the hardships of life in the theatrical profession it had suited her better than that she had led since. She was the kind of woman who exists for admiration, and to whom the approach of middle age is a tragedy. Dancing was the only form of exercise in which she indulged. She hated the country. Collier found her crouching over the fire in her sitting-room.

"I can't think why I have to be worried like this," she began. Collier noted the twitching eyelids and restless hands, with other symptoms of nerves strained to breaking point, and diagnosed the trouble, too much to eat, too many cigarettes, not enough to do, and now this shock. Had she really cared for Stallard?

"I am sorry," he said gently. "If you would just tell me in your own words what you were doing the other evening. Where did you hide?"

"In the drawing-room. I sat on the settee at the far end and smoked a couple of cigarettes. I heard some of them pass through to the conservatory—Angela and those children from the vicarage."

"You did not move until Mr. Darrow gave the alarm?"

"No."

"I don't want to bother you more than I can help," said Collier in his most engaging manner. "I expect you went through all this yesterday with Sergeant Lane. I'm afraid some overlapping is inevitable under the circumstances. This is a difficult and puzzling case, Mrs. Tunbridge. It has some very baffling features, and, to be frank, I need all the help you can give me."

"I know nothing," she said sharply, "but it's fairly obvious, isn't it? I have some valuable jewellery. Some man had got into the house and was concealed in the gallery. Edgar found him and was—was killed in the course of a struggle."

"Some one who knew the house well," said Collier, "well enough to find his way from the gallery to the music-room, up the spiral staircase to the landing above,

and from thence down the service staircase to the servants' quarters. And even then—it doesn't work out, Mrs.
Tunbridge, unless your husband was mistaken. He made
a round of the house before the police arrived and found
every door and window fastened."

"Oh!" She looked at him blankly. "Then I simply can't
imagine—" She shuddered. "It's too horrible. I want to
forget. I can't stand it!" The beautiful face, haggard under
its coat of paint, began to work uncontrollably.

Collier was taking something from his waistcoat pocket.
It was a cigarette holder of Chinese jade. "I know how you
must feel," he said sympathetically. "You've told me all
you can and that's finished." He had got up to go and now
he proffered the holder. "By the way"—Nothing in his tone
betrayed the importance he attached to the question he
was about to ask—"is this yours?"

She shook her head. "No. I haven't got one like that.
Where did you find it?"

He had been watching her closely and he felt fairly sure
that she was telling the truth. The jade holder meant nothing to her. He replaced it in his pocket. "Oh, I picked it up
downstairs," he said casually. "Was Mr. Stallard well off?"

"I don't know. Not very, I imagine."

Her eyes had narrowed. He saw that she was on her
guard again.

"I'll bet he borrowed money from her," he thought.

He thanked her and withdrew to go in search of his
next victim. He found Joan Norris sitting by the fire in her
bedroom, nursing her grief and a cold, a combination that
had obscured her childish prettiness. Collier, who was
usually successful in gaining the confidence of the timid
and downtrodden, soon persuaded her to talk freely. It

was clear that she had taken Stallard's attentions seriously. "He—he—we were together all that last day. He said if
he'd only met me sooner—he said I should teach him to be
a better man. He said such beautiful things—" She began
to cry again.

Collier could imagine the middle-aged amorist saying
them—with his tongue in his cheek. Obviously his intention had been to show Pearl Tunbridge that she must not
be too sure of him, to play off the girl against the woman.

"Don't distress yourself," he said gently. "I just want you
to tell me where you hid when the light was switched off?"

"Oh—in the housemaid's cupboard under the stairs.
There was only room for me with the brooms and brushes.
That's why I chose it. I should have hated to be in a room
where other people could be creeping about. I—I know it's
idiotic, but I'm frightened of the dark. It'll be worse than
ever now. I've had the light on here all night ever since—"

"I see," he said. "Then you hadn't arranged to hide with
Stallard in the gallery?"

"Oh, no. He hadn't asked me," she answered artlessly.

He produced the jade cigarette holder. "Was this Stallard's?"

"I shouldn't think so. No. I remember him saying he
never used one."

"Thank you, Miss Joan. That's something definite, at
any rate."

She lifted terrified eyes. "I want to go home. Can't Barbara and I go home? I shall die if I have to spend another
night in this house."

She had all his attention now. "Why? You're perfectly
safe. No one would hurt you. Your sister sleeps with you,
doesn't she? Do you have your door locked?"

"Yes."

He leaned towards her. "Did you hear anything—last night?"

"I—I thought so. Steps. In the corridor. Barbara was sleeping. I couldn't. I looked at my watch. It was ten minutes past three."

"Well," he said after a pause, "it might have been some one else who couldn't sleep, you know, going down to the library to get a book. That was it, you may depend. As to your going home," he added, "I'll see what can be done."

As he went down the stairs the butler appeared in the hall. "I've been looking for you, Inspector. You're wanted on the phone."

Collier hurried into the library. He had asked the hospital to ring up if Lane recovered consciousness. "How is he?" he began anxiously.

But the voice that answered came from far away. He realized that this was a trunk call. "Who is it speaking?"

The name that was given was that of one of his Chiefs at the Yard. "Yes, sir, Laverne Peveril. I came along this morning. The local man was gassed. An escape of gas. The Superintendent at Parminster and the Chief Constable seemed to think . . . very good, sir . . . In the morning."

Collier hung up the receiver. He was pale under his tan. He should have waited, it seemed, for the official sanction of his superiors before taking charge of the case. Chief Inspector Purley was being sent down to supersede him and was arriving by the afternoon train. He was to supply Purley with all the information he had gathered regarding the crime before he left and to report at headquarters at nine the following morning.

"You're for it, my lad!" he said to himself as he lit a cigarette.

The Chief's tone had been curt. He was evidently annoyed. Suddenly Collier remembered that Sir Eustace had been at the telephone just before lunch. "Of course," he thought. "He rang up to complain of me. He's got a pull there, too. Blast the pompous old fool. He'll smash me, and I was only trying to do my duty." And Purley too! Purley, an older man, who had resented his promotion and was continually finding fault with him. Purley could be trusted to rub salt into his wounds. To Purley his attempts to get people to talk by the exercise of tact and patience seemed merely a display of weakness. "Treat 'em rough!" was his motto and it was certainly his practice. His colleagues knew that he sometimes went very near the border line of what was regarded as permissible in the way of intimidation, and naturally with the professional criminal he was often successful. It remained to be seen, thought Collier, how his browbeating technique would serve him at Laverne Peveril. He wondered, not without a touch of grim amusement, whether in the end Sir Eustace might not regret his interference.

Leaving the library he came face to face with Ruth Clare. The rest of the house party were gathered about the fire at the farther end of the hall having tea, all except Darrow, who was half-way up the stairs. Ruth stopped to speak to the detective and ask for news of Sergeant Lane.

"He hasn't recovered consciousness."

"You look tired out," she said.

"Well, this is a worrying job, Mrs. Clare. I'm not sorry to be through with it."

"Through—" she faltered. He saw her colour fade. "Then you've found—you know—"

He had seen her going down to the lake with Darrow earlier in the day. "She's in love with the fellow," he thought, "and she believes he did it."

"Not that. I've been recalled. Some one else is coming down to take charge. He'll be here any minute now, and when I've given my report I shall be off to catch a train back to Town."

"Oh, what a pity!" she said. "We were getting used to you. Does Mr. Tunbridge know? I'm sure he'll be sorry." She held out her hand.

Collier took it. "You're the only person here who realizes that I don't make a damned nuisance of myself because I like doing it. The whitest man I ever met was an American. Pakenham, his name is. I shan't forget him, and I shan't forget you, Mrs. Clare. If ever I can be of any use to you, call on me. I should be pleased and proud."

Ruth was touched by his evident sincerity. "That's very nice of you. Thank you very much," she said. She forced a smile. It was not easy, for she was desperately anxious and unhappy. She had made a discovery that shattered her faith in the man she had never ceased to love. In the cold light of that new knowledge she dared not even think of those brief moments of ecstasy she had lived through scarcely an hour ago. Finished. Finished. She heard her own voice saying "Good-bye." She went up to her own room, locked the door, and threw herself on the bed. "Oh, Hugh! Hugh! Why didn't you trust me!"

IX
THE NEW BROOM

THE INSPECTOR sent down by Scotland Yard arrived in Colonel Larcombe's motor, and they were accompanied by the Police Superintendent from Parminster. Manners, looking rather flustered, showed them into the little study where Collier awaited them. Purley greeted his colleague with a curt nod, but the other two men were nervously polite.

"A baffling case," said the Chief Constable. "Awkward business altogether. I wish to goodness it hadn't happened. Have you made any progress, Inspector Collier?"

"Not much. I have established that the murder was committed by some one in the house—or by some one with an accomplice in the house. But we knew that before. I found a jade cigarette holder between the cushions on the window seat next to that on which Stallard's body was lying, but I haven't yet discovered the owner. And though Stallard was working on his new book there isn't a scrap of either manuscript or typescript in his room."

Colonel Larcombe pulled at his moustache. "Has that any bearing on the case?"

Purley intervened before Collier could reply. "Very unlikely. Have you found the weapon?"

"I have not."

Purley grunted in a manner that plainly indicated his contempt for the younger man's methods, and Collier reddened. The Chief Constable looked uncomfortable. After all, it was at his request that Collier had given up his holiday to undertake the case.

"It's an awkward business," he repeated, and his tone was apologetic. "Sir Eustace, very naturally, is exceedingly upset, his future wife being here at the time, and all. Most unpleasant and shocking, and I'm afraid, when the Christmas holiday is over, the newspapers will be full of it. Now an ounce of fact, as you said just now in the car coming here, Purley, is worth a pound of theory, but I've been wondering if perhaps a gang of jewel thieves, eh? Mrs. George Tunbridge has some valuable jewellery—"

Collier said nothing. The Superintendent looked at his watch. Colonel Larcombe took the hint. "We'll be getting back. Can we give you a lift to the station, Collier?"

"I have to make my report to Inspector Purley, sir. I've got the motorcycle I borrowed this morning. I can ride back to Parminster on that."

"Very good. We'll be going then. Good night." When they were alone Purley sat down heavily and filled his pipe. "All of a twitter, aren't they? I suppose they'd like this little job hushed up."

Collier shrugged his shoulders. "The Tunbridges are an old county family. If this were the fifteenth century I suppose Stallard's body would have been buried in the park and that would have been the end of it."

Purley paused with an unlighted match in his hand. "You don't think the Tunbridges were in this?"

"I don't know what to think," confessed Collier. "There's the question of motive. Stallard was a hanger-on of Mrs. Tunbridge. He took her out to dinner at restaurants and to dance at night clubs and all that. Mr. George Tunbridge, I gather, gives way to her. But husbands are funny things."

"Any evidence that the two men were on bad terms?"

"None."

"Where was he while this hide and seek foolery was going on?"

"In the hall with young Haviland. They were the seekers."

Purley was pulling at his pipe. "I've seen Lane's first report," he said after a moment. "What was he doing yesterday?"

"I don't know. The notes he made have been removed from his book. If you ask me, Purley, I should say that the turning on of the gas in his bedroom last night was no accident. He should have locked his door."

Purley stared at him. "Can you prove it?"

"No. But, as you can see if you look closely, three leaves have been torn from his notebook. He may have removed them himself, but it isn't very likely."

Purley considered this suggestion in all its bearings. "Hell! If you're right I'm glad I booked a room at the inn before we came up to the house. But I'm not convinced, Collier. You'll forgive my saying that you're a bit too apt to let that imagination of yours run away with you. You seem to have got it into your head that this is a mysterious affair that needs a lot of unravelling. It's a bit beyond you, perhaps, but I fancy I shall get it straightened out before long."

Collier bit his lip. He had expected something like this.

"Well, it's your case now," he said. "Will there be anything more? I ought to be getting along if I'm to catch that train."

"That's all right. Don't let me keep you. Good night."

"Good night," said Collier. He would have liked to add "Don't drop too many bricks!" but he refrained. He could not afford to quarrel with Purley, his senior in the Department. He caught his train with a minute to spare and sat alone in his third-class smoker, staring with unseeing eyes through the misted window-pane into the rayless gloom of the December night. As the express roared through a lighted station he caught a glimpse of the newspaper placards displayed in front of the bookstall.

COUNTRY HOUSE TRAGEDY
MYSTERIOUS DEATH OF WELL-KNOWN AUTHOR

Meanwhile his successor was making his presence felt. Ruth Clare, coming down to the drawing-room where the rest of the party were assembled, found George Tunbridge complaining bitterly.

"I used to think this house was mine, but it doesn't seem to be. The police are all over it, like a plague of blue bottles. Do you hear that hammering?"

"My dear Mr. Tunbridge," said Mrs. Storey in her precise voice. "Nobody here is deaf. What is it?"

"Nothing much. A break-down gang in the boot-room. The two young constables who've been hanging about the place all day are on the job. They're taking up the drains or something. They've cracked the lavatory basin to start with. Collier would at least have asked my permission before he started. But he's gone. A new man who arrived a couple of hours ago is the big noise now. Larcombe brought him."

"Is he on the large side?" enquired Julian Haviland. "I met a human mammoth in the hall just now. He looked at me as if I was something the cat had brought in."

"That sounds like him," said George gloomily. "Collier wasn't so bad, a bit nosy, but you expect that in a detective. I can't understand all this chopping and changing."

Sir Eustace cleared his throat. "As a matter of fact I believe the Yard acted on a hint from me. I rang up this morning after the other man's unwarrantable and uncalled-for attempt to detain me here, and—ah—suggested that they should send down some more competent person."

"Oh!" said his cousin rather blankly. "Well, I think you might have told me. I know you meant well, Eustace, old chap, and all that, but I rather wish you'd let it alone."

"I did what I conceived to be my duty," said Sir Eustace stiffly.

Dinner was an uncomfortable meal. There was an intermittent noise of hammering and a good deal of creaking and shuffling seemed to be going on in the hall. Ruth, increasingly nervous, felt impelled at last to ask a direct question of her host. She was seated on his left, facing Mrs. Storey. "What on earth are they doing, George?"

"Well, the inquest was to have been held at the village hall tomorrow at eleven. This new chap has altered that. It is to be here instead, at two o'clock, in the billiard-room, and the table is being moved out and the carpet taken up, and so forth."

"I see. But what are they doing in the boot-room?" Her voice shook slightly. Tunbridge gave her a quick look.

"Steady," he murmured. "This new chap—he's looking for the knife. He asked me just now if when Darrow came out of the gallery and gave the alarm we searched him. Of course I said we did no such thing. We went into the gallery and saw Stallard. Then I rang up the police. After that Julian and I went all over the house and found all the doors and windows fastened. But as to insulting one of my oldest friends by asking him to turn out his pockets—no!"

She moistened her lips. "Has he—seen Hugh yet?"

"Yes. I was there. He asked Darrow what he did. He said he went to the boot-room and washed his hands. Then he went up to his room and changed from the white Pierrot's dress I had lent him to his blue serge suit and came down again. This fellow Purley asked him why he was in such a hurry to change—"

"Go on," said Ruth.

"He said, 'I knew I'd got into a horrible mess. I felt sick. I hate blood.' Purley wrote that down." She shuddered. "What happened to the Pierrot's suit?"

"The police have got it. Lane took it away. Ruth, don't take it too much to heart. I—I'm sorry now that I pressed you to come down here. Purley wants everybody to stay on until after tomorrow, but you won't be called as a witness, I hope—"

"Are you sure of that?"

"Well—no." He hesitated. "Perhaps I'd better warn you. It seems Angela overheard Darrow say something to you about having a down on Stallard, and she was ass enough to tell the police that. They may want to hear about that from you—"

He looked at her again. She sat pale and silent, crumbling the bread beside her plate with restless fingers.

"Ruth," he said again, earnestly, "I'm most frightfully sorry."

She still said nothing. He turned to Mrs. Storey who was enquiring after his wife.

"Better, thank you, but it'll take her a little time to get over the shock. She's fearfully highly strung, you know."

"Nerves," said Mrs. Storey, "tiresome things, I am sure. I haven't any myself. But I don't belong to this age. Rushing about in speeding cars, jazz, cocktails and cigarettes are hardly the best preparation for shocks when they come. And little Miss Joan? Is she nervous too? I don't see her here."

"She's got a bad cold," explained George. "Her sister thought she'd better stay in bed."

"Very wise," Mrs. Storey helped herself to the sweet. Unlike Ruth, she had made an excellent dinner. She was, on her own admission, a person of restricted sympathies. "I'm too old to worry over other folk's troubles. It's very sad, of course, but—"

"I suppose the young people mustn't dance," she said now, "it wouldn't be quite decent, would it? But there can't be any objection to a game of bridge."

"I suppose not," said George with an attempt at heartiness. He did not really enjoy playing with Mrs. Storey. She was so much too good for him. But, "Poor old soul!" he thought. "It's her only amusement."

Mrs. Storey leaned forward to call Ruth's attention. "You will play, Mrs. Clare? We shall want you—"

Ruth started. Her thoughts had been elsewhere. "Oh—not tonight, please! I—I've got a headache."

Mrs. Storey's fine old face expressed polite incredulity. "After all that exercise and fresh air? What a pity."

George intervened. "Diana and I will play you and Eustace, Mrs. Storey. You'll wipe the floor with us, but we're used to it."

Later, he went up to his wife's room. Pearl was sitting up in bed propped with pillows, smoking cigarettes and reading a novel which she laid down as he entered.

"Well?" Her voice, one of those drawling treacly husky voices that are so effective on the stage, betrayed nervous tension.

George groaned. "You're well out of it up here. I'm sick of all these people. Thank God, most of them will be going tomorrow. I've got to go down and play bridge now. That old woman is a terror. Still we've got to pass the time somehow. It's like a damned nightmare."

"Poor old boy. But we'll get off soon, won't we? Right out of England for a bit," she said eagerly.

He sighed. "All right, Pearl. Yes. You generally get your way, don't you?"

X
THE INQUEST OPENS

THERE WAS still a feeling of snow in the air but only a few flakes had fallen from a leaden sky when the inquest on Edgar Stallard was opened by the deputy coroner for the district, sitting with a jury, in the billiard room of Laverne Peveril. Rags Norris nudged his friend Bunny as old Veale, who kept the general shop in the village, was elected foreman. He had discussed this probability with his sister Barbara before lunch, in the course of a walk round the park with the Havilands.

"If he's foreman we're for it," opined Rags, not without a certain relish. "He's got his knife into Dad for Popish practices and encouraging dancing and allowing Joan to raffle her white rabbit at the bazaar last summer. Do the Tunbridges deal with him?"

"I shouldn't think so," said Angela. "Pearl gets things from the Stores."

"Then we're all as good as dead!" said Rags solemnly. His sister stopped him. "Shut up! You're not a bit funny. I wish it was over."

But the five young people, as they walked on together under the trees, had not been able to refrain from talking about the crime.

"I suppose it's really pretty obvious," said Rags regretfully. "If he could see there'd be no doubt at all. As it is his counsel will have to make the most of the impossibility of a blind man striking in a vital spot at the first go. I mean—I don't want to be flippant—but have you ever tried to pin a tail on to a paper donkey with your eyes bandaged? If there had been a hand-to-hand struggle it would be different. But—I expect you all noticed—that tulle ruffle round Darrow's neck wasn't torn or tumbled."

"I noticed," said Angela. "I made it for him. He's nice in a low-spirited under-the-weather sort of way. It's a thousand pities that garden door was locked. We could all have sworn that we'd seen a suspicious-looking man lurking about."

"I say!" exclaimed Bunny. "You never told us that before. Do the police know?"

"I've only just invented him," said Angela coolly.

"Have you noticed how Mrs. Clare has altered just lately?" enquired Rags Norris, after a pause. "She looked so ill and depressed last night, and she didn't come down to breakfast this morning."

"Well, it's rotten for her," said Barbara. Later, when she was alone with her brother, she asked him if he had remarked that from the moment they left the house until they returned Julian Haviland had not uttered a word. "Rather funny, I thought."

Rags looked at her. "Are you suggesting that he did the job?"

"Well—we don't know, do we?"

It was that terrible uncertainty that was wearing them all down. They did not know. Barbara voiced another feeling that was probably general.

"I shouldn't have felt it to be so horrible that the criminal is still at large, sitting down to meals with us, rubbing shoulders, if Stallard had been shot. I mean—a knife is so much more savage and merciless—"

Young Norris recalled his sister's words as he watched the coroner looking round the court over the tops of his glasses as if to gain some idea of his audience before he began. One advantage of holding the inquest at the house was that the general public could be excluded, and the billiard-room was not overcrowded. Ruth Clare and Angela Haviland sat together and were, with Mrs. Gore, the housekeeper, and Miss Berry, the head housemaid, the only women present, but there were representatives not only of the Parminster *Herald and Argus* but of all the London daily papers at the Press table, and it was clear that the Laverne Peveril mystery was to get its full share of publicity henceforward.

The coroner cleared his throat. "Now, gentlemen, you have already viewed the body of the unfortunate gentleman in the coach house at the back of the White Hart before coming on here, and Inspector Purley has just conducted you through the gallery in which that body was found. I am sorry that you have had to be called away from your homes at this festive season, but it was necessary. I shall only call two or three witnesses before we adjourn indefinitely, leaving the police to pursue their investigations into this tragic affair—" He broke off as Purley, who was standing at his elbow, stooped and whispered in his ear. "Oh—not indefinitely—we may be prepared for early developments. Now I will state the facts quite briefly. Mr. Stallard, who is an author, was one of the guests invited to Laverne Peveril by Mr. Tunbridge for Christmas week. On Monday night everyone appeared at dinner in fancy dress. After dinner all the servants except one chauffeur, who went to bed with face-ache, went off in a bus to the village hall to a dance. Meanwhile Mr. and Mrs. Tunbridge and their guests played hide and seek all over the house. The electric light was turned off at the main and for nearly thirty minutes the place was in darkness. During that time, gentlemen, murder was done, and we are met here to find out, if we can, how, and by whom. As to how I shall now call Dr. Henshawe, the police surgeon who saw the deceased the same night before the body was moved from where it lay. Dr. Henshawe."

The doctor rose in his place and took the oath. He described his arrival between half past ten and eleven.

"The body was lying on the cushioned window seat. The hands were gripping the ledge. There was no sign of a struggle. I should say that the deceased was taken by surprise. The wound was three inches deep and had penetrated the heart. Death must have been practically instantaneous."

"Might the wound have been self-inflicted?"

The doctor seemed to hesitate. "Yes. But then I should expect to find the weapon either in the wound or close by, dropped from the dead man's hand."

"Quite. One thing more. Stabs in the region of the chest are not necessarily fatal?"

"Oh, no."

"Would you say that whoever struck this blow showed some knowledge of anatomy?"

"Well—perhaps—yes."

"Thank you. That will do for the present, Dr. Henshawe. I will now call Mr. Hugh Darrow." There was a great stillness in the room as Darrow stood up and waited for a policeman to lead him forward. He repeated the words of the oath in a low voice but distinctly.

"Now, Mr. Darrow, will you tell us in your own words how you found Mr. Stallard's body."

"I lingered in the hall for some time after the lights had been put out and the rest of the party had dispersed to find hiding places. I did not really want to join in the game. Finally I decided to go into the gallery and wait in one of the window embrasures. I went to the first on the right. The gong was sounded fairly soon afterwards but the seekers did not enter the gallery—"

"One moment. Who were the seekers?"

"Mr. Tunbridge and Mr. Haviland."

"Thank you. What happened then?"

"I heard a dripping noise. I should explain that my sense of hearing is more acute since I lost my sight. There was something sinister about it. It seemed to come from the embrasure opposite. I went over and felt about with my hands. That was how I got all smeared with blood—"

"Is that all, Mr. Darrow?"

"I rushed out of the gallery and gave the alarm."

The coroner was writing down the replies to his questions. His pen scratched away in the silence. No one moved. Presently he looked up again.

"Anything more, Mr. Darrow? You are on your oath, remember."

"Yes. There is something. When I first entered the gallery I fancied there was somebody there. I thought I heard breathing and a faint whispering and then a breath of colder air as if a door or window had been opened."

"Why haven't you mentioned this before, Mr. Darrow?"

"I wasn't sure. My impression at the time was that there was a man—and a woman. It was only an impression."

"I see. What is your profession, Mr. Darrow?"

"Well, I was an art student when the war broke out. Now I have my pension and I do a bit of hand weaving and basket work."

"An art training would include some knowledge of anatomy?"

"Yes."

"You have been blind for a considerable time?"

"The trench I was in was blown up on the eighteenth of October, nineteen-seventeen. I lost my sight then."

"Irreparably? I mean, you are stone blind?"

"The doctors thought I might regain my sight. A shock might do it."

"For instance, the shock of an unexpected meeting with a man you hated?"

"They didn't say what kind of shock."

"You are no longer blind?"

The heart of one of his listeners seemed to miss a beat and then go racing on. To her the long pause that ensued was an agony. By now everyone present was aware of what was being implied and the atmosphere of the room was electric. The answer came at length.

"No."

"You have been shamming blindness. Just now you allowed the policeman to lead you to the table. Have you any explanation to offer?"

"I told you I rushed into the hall. I found that when George—Mr. Tunbridge—switched the lights on I could see. I was so excited that for the moment I hardly realized what had happened. Everybody was frightfully agitated, running about. It was like an ant's nest when you poke it with a stick. They were thinking about Stallard, and getting the police, and I—there was blood on my hands and on my sleeves. I felt sick. Oh, God!"

There was another dreadful pause. The coroner whispered to Purley who signed to a policeman to take the witness a glass of water. Darrow took it with a word of thanks and drank thirstily. It was noticed that his hand shook so that some water was spilled.

"Can you go on now, Mr. Darrow?"

"Yes. I washed my hands in the boot-room, and then I went upstairs and changed into the suit I'm wearing now and came down again just as the police arrived. Tunbridge had lent me the Pierrot costume. I don't know what happened to it. I left it on the floor in my room and I didn't see it again."

"The police took possession of it. Anything more, Mr. Darrow? Sergeant Lane took a statement from you that evening. We have it here in a transcription from his shorthand notes. How do you account for the fact that you said nothing to him about your recovered sight?"

"I should have done. I realize that now. The truth is I funked it. It meant a lot of explaining and I was afraid he wouldn't believe me. I dreaded a fuss and a lot of questions."

"A great pity," said the coroner. "However—do you wish to say anything at this stage in the proceedings regarding your relations with the deceased?"

"I had no relations with him. I never met him before."

The coroner looked at the witness over his glasses. "Be careful, Mr. Darrow. You can decline to answer questions—but if you do answer I should advise you to be quite candid. You were heard to use some rather violent language concerning the dead man, to express enmity—do you deny that?"

"No."

The silence in the room was profound. Ruth Clare, looking down at her clenched hands, saw the handkerchief she had been holding in rags. Unconsciously she had torn it to ribbons while she sat there, helpless, watching the net drawn closer.

"Do you care to amplify that answer?"

"Perhaps I had better. During the war my half-sister was in Egypt. She was a V.A.D. Stallard was out there in some official capacity, and he made love to her. She became infatuated with him, and—he should have married her, but he didn't. She shot herself. It was hushed up and there was no scandal. He was useful, I suppose. I was in France at the time, but I heard the story later from one of her fellow nurses. That's why I used—rather violent language, as you say—when I learned that we were fellow guests here."

The coroner held a whispered consultation with Purley before he resumed.

"I think, Mr. Darrow, that you should be legally represented. In order to give you time to make the necessary arrangements I propose to adjourn this enquiry for a week."

"Just a minute, Mr. Coroner." Mr. Veale, the village grocer, lumbered to his feet. "We'd like to know, me and the jury, before we goes home, why the Parminster police ambulance came up here yesterday morning? It's made a lot of talk down the village."

"Certainly, Mr. Foreman. Sergeant Lane, of the Parminster division, was in charge of the case, and Mr. Tunbridge had very kindly placed a bedroom at his disposal so that he might be on the spot during the preliminary stages of his investigation. Unfortunately the tap of the gas fire in the room was left partly turned on, and the sergeant was found in the morning unconscious, suffering from carbon monoxide poison, and had to be removed to the Parminster cottage hospital, where I understand that he is progressing as well as can be expected."

"Then it was just an accident like?"

The coroner glanced up at Purley who bent down to say something.

"So far as we know at present purely an accident. Is that all, Mr. Foreman?"

"Yes, sir."

"Then we will adjourn."

XI
ENTER GLIDE

COLONEL LARCOMBE, who had been watching the snowflakes whirling down from the library window, turned back into the room where Inspector Purley stood with his back to the fire, smoking a cigar.

"I doubt if you'd get him away tonight with this weather," he observed.

Purley grunted. "It'd take more than a fall of snow to stop me." The house was quieter now than it had been all day. The jurymen had departed in the same bus that had been hired from the White Hart a few nights earlier to take the servants to the dance. The coroner had driven off in his two-seater, and the vicar, whose stipend did not admit of his keeping any kind of conveyance, had trudged away on foot across the park with his party of boys and girls. The house was quieter, but its atmosphere was no less tense. Its silence had a sinister quality. It seemed to be waiting for a blow to fall.

Purley glanced round with a frown as George Tunbridge and Mrs. Clare entered the library. Colonel Larcombe cleared his throat nervously. "We'll be leaving soon, Mr. Tunbridge. Meanwhile, don't you think—"

George came directly to the point. "Mrs. Clare has got it into her head that you think of arresting Darrow. I wish you'd reassure her."

"I am not prepared to discuss my conduct of this case with any but my superiors at Scotland Yard, Mr. Tunbridge. Will you take the lady away? If she wishes to help Mr. Darrow I should advise her to engage a good lawyer and be guided by him."

"We shall do that, of course," said George, not without dignity. "My dear, come along. It's no use." Ruth said nothing until they were in the hall, the library door closed behind them. Then she turned to her companion with sparkling eyes. "What time does the four-twelve from Waterloo get into Parminster?"

"At five-forty-five. It is one of the fastest trains of the day. Why?"

She glanced at her wrist watch. "Then he ought to be here soon. He was coming by that. If only he didn't miss it. It must have been a rush."

George was staring. "What on earth are you talking about?"

"Why, I rang up my nice Inspector Collier directly after the inquest. I was near the door and got out first. I told him how bad it looked for Hugh and that he was going to need some one to stand up for him. He said he couldn't do a thing himself but if I liked he'd send a private detective, and should he ring him up and see if he could come. So I said yes, and waited, and I was in a fever because I knew the police might want to telephone. However, after I'd held on about ten minutes he came back and said that the man he had in mind was prepared to undertake the job and would catch the four-twelve. I hope you don't mind, George? I ought to have told you before."

"That's all right," said George. "You acted for the best. I must tell Manners. What's the chap's name?"

"I'm not sure. You know what these trunk calls are! I only heard half what he said. It sounded like Glide."

"Well, there's plenty of room here," said George, wondering what Pearl would say of another invader. "We could house a regiment of detectives at Laverne—but I must say I hope that won't be necessary." He broke off as his cousin came out of the drawing-room. "Hallo, Eustace."

"I've been settling the time of our departure with Diana," said the baronet, "immediately after breakfast to-morrow." He did not renew his invitation to Ruth to take her back to Town.

"Weather permitting," said George.

"Is there any doubt of that?"

"Well—it's snowing hard. You may need chains by the morning." Ruth moved away. "I shall be in the drawing-room, George."

Sir Eustace looked after her with unwilling admiration. "She holds herself well. But I don't altogether approve of her. I don't like to see a woman make herself cheap. Can't you give her a hint to be more careful and keep away from Darrow?" George answered gruffly. "No, I can't. I hope I may have as loyal a friend if ever I'm in a hole." Eustace was on his way upstairs to dress for dinner. George, who had changed early, lingered in the hall. He might as well get an early view of the latest on the lengthening list of investigators into the mystery surrounding the death of Edgar Stallard. He had not long to wait. He heard the arrival of a car and went himself to open the door. He had to lean against it to close it for the wind was rising to a gale and a white scurry of snow had blown in with the visitor. George was surprised. Somehow he had expected to see a big man. But the head of the newcomer barely reached his shoulder.

"My name is Glide, Hermann Glide. You were expecting me?" Ruth came out of the drawing-room and joined them before George could answer.

"Where can we talk without being interrupted, George?"

"God knows," said the master of the house resignedly. "Manners will be in and out of the dining-room. Scotland Yard is in possession of the library. The other chap, Collier, made do with the little study, but Purley seemed to think it wasn't large enough. Perhaps it may do for us. This way, Mr. Glide."

In the study, with its framed photographs of favourite horses and dogs and its untidy piles of bulb catalogues and back numbers of *Country Life*, they sat down, before the old-fashioned steel fender and George passed round his cigarette case. Mr. Glide, however, declined to smoke. "Another time, perhaps. Just now I want to keep my head clear."

He had removed a thick overcoat and a woollen muffler and revealed a lamentably narrow chest and a wizened little face, pinched with cold and lit by a pair of brilliant and melancholy brown eyes. He looked, Ruth thought, exactly like a sick monkey. Even his hands, with their long delicate fingers—but what was he doing with them?

He smiled at her, seeing her perplexity, and his smile was oddly attractive. "This is a lump of modelling wax. I carry it about with me everywhere. I find that to work it aids my mental processes. You want me to find the murderer here?"

"Not so much that," said Ruth, "that's for the police. I want you to prove Mr. Darrow's innocence."

"Who is employing me? I must know the exact position."

"I am," she said quickly.

"I have read the newspaper reports. You must tell me a great deal more. The inquest was opened this afternoon and adjourned."

Ruth told him. Now and again he helped her with a question. George sat by, smoking.

All the while the thin fingers worked busily kneading the grey wax to strange forms that merged into others and vanished.

"That's all, I think," she said at last.

There was a silence. Glide's bright brown eyes seemed to be searching the glowing caverns in the heart of the fire.

"Yes," he said at last, "Inspector Collier, who is a friend of mine, seemed to fear that there might be a miscarriage of justice in this case. I'm glad I came. It's very interesting. Well, Mrs. Clare, I'll clear the ground to begin with by saying that my terms are ten guineas a week and expenses. You'll have to pay just the same if I prove your friend's guilt. You understand that? I may be unscrupulous in my methods of getting at the truth. They say I am. But when I've found it I don't palter with it." He glanced at her in time to see the colour flood her pale cheeks.

"I'm not afraid of the truth," she said steadily.

"Very good. Then I'll get to work at once. I'll just have a look round the gallery to begin with. When do you dine here?"

George replied as the question was addressed to him. "At eight."

XII
THE EVE OF DEPARTURE

MRS. STOREY had been resting but she was awake when her granddaughter came into her room, which, as usual, was rather airless and smelt faintly of eau de cologne and moth balls.

She turned her small withered face quickly in the direction of the door as Diana lingered.

"Come in, child. There's a draught." She spoke sharply. Proud as she was of the girl's beauty she was often very impatient with her when they were alone. Their fellow guests at the cheap private hotel in Earl's Court where they had stayed in the interval between their return from Cannes and their coming to Laverne Peveril were sometimes rather sorry for her granddaughter.

"Eustace says we are to leave here tomorrow about nine," said Diana.

"Very well. I hope Sir Eustace still intends to take us to the Savoy. It's a good thing we met him when we did, Diana. I hope you realize that ever since you left the convent school at Versailles last spring I have been living far beyond my means. I was determined to give you a chance to meet the right sort of people. I was prepared to make sacrifices, considerable sacrifices, for your sake."

"Yes, Grandma."

Diana had heard all this before and her assent was purely mechanical. She always agreed with her grandmother. It made life so much easier. Mrs. Storey considered that Diana had done very well indeed. Sir Eustace could give her everything a woman wants. He would make an excellent husband, a trifle boring certainly, but it was easy to acquire the art of appearing to listen while not actually doing so, and Diana would have been considered dull herself if she had not been so exceedingly good to look at.

"I don't care for London in January, but we can begin to get your trousseau. What happened at the inquest? Did Eustace tell you?"

"Yes. He says there's no doubt that Mr. Darrow did it. He gave his evidence and admitted that he wasn't blind now. He said the shock of finding the body brought his sight back, but Eustace said he could see nobody believed him. He thought the police were taking him away this evening."

"Dear me!" said Mrs. Storey. "How very unpleasant it all is. Diana, I have been thinking that in view of all this it might be best for you to be married quietly and sooner than we originally planned. Then Eustace can take you abroad for a long honeymoon, and you'll escape the disagreeable publicity in which you might be involved if the enquiry is protracted."

"I'd rather not be married before Easter," said Diana, and her lovely face assumed what her grandmother called her mulish expression.

"You'll do what I think best," said Mrs. Storey.

"I'd rather not," said Diana again in the cool precise little voice that was like an echo of her grandmother's.

"Rubbish! As a matter of fact I sounded Eustace last night. One has to be careful with a man like that who has been tremendously run after all his life. However, it was all right. He is quite willing. He sees that a big wedding would be undesirable under the circumstances, and he is going to make the necessary arrangements. I thought about the tenth of January. That will give us time to get your clothes."

Diana stood, looking down like a sulky child, and twisting the diamond ring on her finger. She knew that when her grandmother spoke in that brisk decided tone it was useless for her to contend. Mrs. Storey, satisfied by her silence, dropped the subject. "Run along, child. It's time you dressed for dinner. I shall not come down. Tell them to send me up something on a tray. Say good night to me now. I daresay I shall be asleep when you come up to bed."

Diana bent over her dutifully and touched the wrinkled cheek with her fresh young lips.

"Good night, my darling. You know it is all for your sake, don't you? I want you to be happy, to have all the things that I missed when I was your age. All these years I have planned and dreamed for you, and now my dreams are coming true. Good night."

"Yes, Grandma."

Diana passed into her own room and went to her wardrobe. She had five evening frocks, only one of which had been paid for. The bills for the others would be sent in when she was safely married. Mrs. Storey had told Colette that she would have to wait for her money, and the dressmaker, when she had verified the fact of her customer's engagement to Sir Eustace Tunbridge, had been all smiles and eagerness. "Why not take the white and silver also? It would suit mademoiselle, being so fair."

Diana, who loved her pretty clothes, passed her hands caressingly down the soft shining folds and chose her favourite, a rose-coloured velvet that fitted her slender body like a sheath and flared out at the hips into flounces of lace of the same shade. Only ten minutes to have her bath and change. She would be late, but it was better so. The others would be in the dining-room when she went down. She would have to sit in her usual place next to Eustace, of course, but he never talked much at dinner, he was too busy with his food. She saw herself in the glass as she hastily passed a comb through her golden curls. She was perhaps a little pale, but not noticeably different.

In fact, no one paid much attention to her throughout the meal. Pearl had come down for the first time. She looked worn and ill in spite of her elaborate make-up and was inclined to be snappy with her husband and Angela Haviland. Ruth Clare was white and silent. Julian Haviland earned everybody's gratitude by holding forth in a high cheerful voice on a variety of subjects chosen at random and including dirt-track racing, the advantages of the Balearic Isles as a winter resort, and the composition of a cocktail of his own invention.

"It was heroic," his sister told him later. "No one listened, but all were thankful for the barrage. I say, who was that queer little man taking the parlourmaid's place by the sideboard? I thought I knew all the servants indoors and out."

"Lord knows!" said Julian. He was lying on a sofa in the drawing-room, exhausted by his efforts. They were alone for the moment.

"I say, Angela, are we going to be asked to stay on?"

"I am. Pearl finds me useful. And she's giving me a fur coat for a Christmas present. George is going to take her to Monte as soon as they can get away and she's half promised to take me, too."

"And me," said Julian. "She'll need a dancing partner, won't she?"

"I'll try and work it," his sister promised. "Perhaps I can appeal to George's patriotism. Better you than some foreigner. Patronize home industries!" She shivered, glancing round the vast deserted drawing-room. "The sooner the better. This place feels like a vault. I miss those kids from the vicarage."

Julian reached for another cushion and arranged it carefully under his head. "Yes. I detest heartiness as a rule, but even the loud laugh that proceeds from the vacant mind has its uses in a house infested by policemen, with a murderer still at large."

Angela lowered her voice. "Did you see Darrow go away with the Inspector? I peeped over the stairs. George and Mrs. Clare were in the hall and they both shook hands with him. They seem to believe in him—but if he didn't do it, who did?"

"Exactly. It's not as if it was a hateful and unnatural crime," argued her brother. "I mean, Stallard had rather asked for it, hadn't he? One can think Darrow was the man, and yet retain quite a liking for him."

"Yes—" said his sister doubtfully, "I suppose so. But there's something about a knife."

Julian agreed. "I know. Silly to be squeamish, but I don't care for butchers myself. I'd rather not shake hands with him. Must be a repression—or mustn't it?" He yawned. "Where's everybody? Where's the wax doll? If I had to choose one of Hoffman's lady friends it wouldn't be the one in the first act."

Angela smiled but said nothing. Her eyes were very sharp, and chance had put her in possession of some very exclusive information about Diana which she was not disposed to share just yet with anyone.

XIII
ESCAPE

A PART OF the stables at Laverne Peveril had been converted for the use of cars. Sir Eustace Tunbridge's big Rolls-Royce was garaged in what had been a coach house, and the chauffeur slept in the harness-room which was reached from the paved yard by means of a flight of brick steps, overgrown with Virginia creeper and flanked by a big stone which was still used, when the local hunt met at Laverne Peveril, as a mounting block.

Ivan Pavlovski spent a good deal of his spare time in his room, for his surroundings were strange to him and the gossip of his fellow servants bored him. Justine, too, had been troublesome. She was like a cat waiting for a chance to scratch.

He was sitting on the foot of his bed, polishing his black leather leggings with an oily rag and whistling the Habanera when the door burst open and a little bedraggled figure stumbled in.

"Ivan—"

"Diana!" He sprang up and caught her in his arms.

The rose-coloured velvet, the golden curls were dank with half-melted snow, the lace flounces hung bedraggled. "Chérie, are you mad to come like this, without a wrap! What has happened? Is it safe?"

"I told Eustace I was going up to bed. No one will expect to see me again tonight. I had to come! Ivan, kiss me! Again!"

He held her close, his lean hands gripping her bare arms, his lips seeking hers, exulting as he felt her response. "Ma chérie. Mon amour—"

He sat down again and drew her on to his knees. "Now tell me."

"I'm to be married the tenth of January. Grandma has arranged it with Eustace. Ivan, I can't bear it. I can't go through with it."

He held her so tightly that she could hardly breathe. "Ivan, you're hurting me!"

"I don't care. Are you coming away with me?"

"Yes."

"You understand what it means? I am poor. I have nothing to offer but all my heart. I must go back to driving a taxi. We shall have to live in one room, and you will cook the meals and wash my shirts." They both laughed. It did not sound real. Nothing was real at that moment except their passion.

Until tonight, though she met him secretly as often as it could be contrived, she had always talked of their love as hopeless and her marriage as inevitable. He was unprepared, but he began to make plans. They could meet in London. "I don't know your marriage laws. There will be formalities—"

She interrupted. "Grandma will find out and stop it. She could. I'm only eighteen and you're a foreigner. Her consent would be needed. It's too difficult. And she—you don't know, Ivan. I can't stand up against her. And he'll be hurt and angry—"

The young Russian nodded gloomily. "I know. He will have the right to be. We have not treated him well, Diana."

"He is so stupid," she said, as if that settled it. "Listen, Ivan. If you want me you must take me now, tonight."

"Tonight! But that is impossible."

"We can go to Parminster in the Rolls and leave it there."

"Mon Dieu!" The young man laughed in spite of himself. "In his automobile. Would not that be—how do you say?—seething the kid in his mother's milk?"

"Don't be silly, dearest, and don't waste time. I want to go now, before I have time to get frightened." She pointed to the chest of drawers. "Are your things in there? I'll stuff them into your bag while you get the car out."

"But what about you? You can't run away in a pink velvet frock and silver slippers," he objected.

"I didn't think of running away before dinner when I was changing," she explained, "and I was afraid to go up afterwards and get a coat because of Grandma. I can buy some clothes tomorrow. I've got the gold cigarette case Eustace gave me for my birthday in my little bag and we ought to be able to raise quite a lot of money on my ring."

The Russian was amused and perhaps just a little shocked but he was too much in love to be very critical. He yielded against his better judgment. After all, since he was robbing his employer of his promised wife the borrowing of his car for an hour or two was a minor wrong that would hardly weigh in the scale, and there would be no need to pawn her engagement ring. He would see that she sent it back the next day. He had been careful and had saved a few pounds out of his wages, enough to tide them over two or three weeks.

"Very well," he said, "you shall pack for me while I get the car out. You can wear my overcoat over all this. I know some Russians in London who will take us in if we can get up tonight."

What would they say, what would they think, these people whom they were leaving for ever? He neither knew nor cared just then. Diana's lashes fluttered against his cheek, he could feel the beating of her heart under his hand. Nothing else mattered.

Now that the die was cast he was seized with a fear that they would be stopped. He would not let her pack for him. It took him less than five minutes to hurl his few belongings into his bag. He made her wear his fleece-lined chauffeur's overcoat and tied one of his scarves over her head.

Then they switched off the light and felt their way down the steps to the yard.

Even here, with the house to shelter them, the icy wind cut their faces and the whirling snowflakes took their breath. Ivan opened the garage doors. The great car stood within, ready for the road. He would have to drive her in the dark until they got clear of the house, for the powerful headlights shining through the kitchen windows across the yard would be certain to attract attention. He helped the girl in and started very carefully, guided by the black bulk of the house on his left, through the arched gateway and round by the terrace.

"What was that?" asked the girl as they bumped over something.

"Probably a flowerbed. I can't keep to the road with this snow. I thought I could follow the tracks of the cars that left earlier, but they are covered."

They were well away from the house now and he took the risk of turning on the headlights, but they pierced only a little way into the blackness in which flakes danced as motes dance in a beam of sunshine, with a kind of remote and unearthly gaiety that dazes and bewilders the watcher.

"These must be the trees of the avenue. Will they open the lodge gates for us?"

He was staring anxiously through the glass, his dark eyes strained to see the obstacles that loomed up before them, tree trunks, shrubberies bowed down with the weight of their burden of snow. He knew now that they had been mad to make the attempt on such a night, but there could be no turning back. Had they left the avenue? Should he bear more to the right? He turned in that direction and scraped the bole of an oak whose overhanging branches rattled like small shot over the roof of the car.

"Are we all right, Ivan?"

"I hope so, chérie."

He thought of the tyres and wished he had chains. If they ran into a drift what could they do? He muttered something in his own language that might have been a prayer to the saints who watch over the reckless as another tree towered up in their path and he made a sharp turn to avoid it. They were off the avenue, they must be, but they seemed to have got clear of the trees. He accelerated and then tried to slow down as he realized that the slope they were on was far too steep. But the brakes failed to act and the car was carried forward by her own momentum, slithering helplessly like some huge animal over a bank on to a flat white surface that splintered and crashed under their weight.

Diana screamed. "The lake! The lake!"

The lights of the car went out as she heeled slowly over sideways, sinking into the mud as the black ice-cold water came bubbling up through the jagged hole she had made. Ivan felt the girl's body that had been stiff with terror, go slack in his arms as she lost consciousness. He struck upwards, trying to break the glass of the window, and, shattering it, cut his wrist to the bone. Water was pouring in on them. Would they be drowned like rats in a trap?

XIV
"SHE IS MINE!"

It had been a long and tiring day and George Tunbridge, comfortably ensconced in his favourite armchair by the library fire, had been lulled into a gentle doze by the monotonous flow of his cousin's voice. The words Government, education, tariffs, economy, drifted by him like leaves floating on a stream whose surface is smooth. Underneath the current ran darkly, bearing burdens he wanted to forget. Pearl was making an effort to pull herself together. He would take her abroad. How far had she gone with that bounder? Better not think of it.

He sat up abruptly and Sir Eustace broke off in the middle of a sentence. Some one had entered the room swiftly. Sir Eustace, turning his head, saw a wizened little man in a dark suit.

"Who is this, George?"

The little man answered him directly. "My name is Glide. I am a detective engaged on this case. Is it by your orders, Sir Eustace, that your chauffeur has taken your car out?"

"My chauffeur? Certainly not."

Glide's quick brown eyes had seen the telephone. "Are you connected with the lodge, Mr. Tunbridge? Good. Then I'll ring up the lodgekeeper and tell him not to open the gates. Or—perhaps you'd better do it yourself."

Obediently George took up the receiver. "What the hell—however—hallo—hallo—is that you, Jenkins? Keep the gates closed until you hear again from me. No one is to pass out. No one. Is Sir Eustace's Rolls waiting to go out now? Very well." He hung up the receiver. "Now, Mr. Glide, my lodgekeeper says—"

The telephone bell rang sharply and he went back to the instrument. "What? Oh—that's queer. Yes, better find out—"

He turned back to the others. "He says he saw a flash of light a few minutes ago in the direction of the lake. It's gone now. I told him to take Williams, one of the under-gardeners who lodges with him, and a lanthorn, and see what's up."

"There must be some mistake," said Sir Eustace. "Ivan would never take my car out on such a night. Besides, why should he? It's absurd."

Glide was not listening. "I don't like this," he said. "They should have reached the lodge by now. Will you get on your overcoats, gentlemen, and come with me? Manners is too old to be of much use. We'd better have Mr. Haviland if we can get him quickly. There's not a moment to lose."

"Not until I have ascertained for myself that my car has been taken out," said Sir Eustace. "I refuse to be led out on a wild goose chase by a complete stranger." He rang the bell vigorously.

"Meanwhile I will fetch my coat," said Glide, "and put on my galoshes. I am glad I brought them. I am subject to colds."

The baronet was the type of man who expresses un-certainty and alarm by blustering. "Who is this extraor-dinary person, George, and who gave him leave to order us about? Ah, here's Manners. Manners, my car is in the garage, of course?"

The old butler glanced from him to his master. "I'm sorry, sir. I can't say I heard her go myself. It's not above ten minutes. Two of the maids that were washing up in the scullery saw her move out. Not plain, of course, on account of the darkness and the snow, but plain enough. I'm very sorry about it, sir, with all the trouble there's been in the house already."

The Tunbridges were both staring at him. George spoke first. "I don't understand. You seem to know more about this than we do, Manners."

The butler looked back at them unhappily. "I didn't think—" He cleared his throat. "I didn't think they'd proceed to extremes," he faltered.

Sir Eustace took a step towards him. "Speak plainly, can't you!"

Before the old man could reply Glide came back. He was followed by Julian Haviland carrying an armful of coats. Glide himself had a lanthorn. "Quickly, please," he said sharply, "I'm afraid the chauffeur lost his way. There's probably been some kind of smash. This is a rescue party. There'll be plenty of time to talk later."

They followed without further demur. He led them out of the house into the icy stillness of the night. The wind had fallen suddenly and the air that had been full of whirling snowflakes was black and empty as a vast frozen grave. The two Tunbridges and Haviland plodded in the wake of the lanthorn across the unbroken white surface and stopped when its bearer stopped.

"You see," Glide expounded, "the tyre marks. He missed the avenue here and got on to the grass. What is there at the foot of this slope?"

George answered. "The lake. It's frozen over. We've been skating—"

"Listen," said Haviland.

"We're wasting time. We must follow the tracks."

Glide started off down the slope, the others close at his heels. As they came past the belt of trees that screened the lake from above George Tunbridge exclaimed. "There's a light down there now!"

"The two men from the lodge have got there first," said Glide. There was relief in his voice. Just then the eldest of the party, Sir Eustace, stumbled over a tree stump. George stopped to help him up while Glide and young Haviland pushed on.

Haviland took his opportunity. "What are we after, anyway?"

"You'll see soon enough now."

There was no time for more. The other two came plunging down the slope after them, and they were together when they reached their goal.

The big car lay almost completely submerged among the reeds at the edge of the lake. The lodge-keeper knelt on the bank, holding his lanthorn at arm's length to cast as much light as possible through the shattered window to the interior. The gardener clung precariously to the roof while he helped a third man to lift something out.

"What is it?" asked Sir Eustace loudly.

No one answered him. There was no need. They knew that he must have seen what they all saw, the golden head hanging inert, like a broken flower from its stem, and have realized, as they all did, whose body it was that the Russian chauffeur carried as, helped on either side by his rescuers, he staggered up the bank towards them.

George Tunbridge's voice, high-pitched and quavering, broke the shocked silence.

"You—you scoundrel! What have you done to her? Is she—dead?"

The Russian said nothing. His face was white and dazed. Blood was dripping on the snow from his cut wrist. Once again Glide took the lead, issuing orders that were instinctively obeyed.

When they reached the house the butler, who had been waiting in the hall, admitted them.

"Get brandy, and something to bind up the man's wrist. The young lady will have to be put to bed," said Glide. He turned to George. "We want somebody with a cool head and some knowledge of nursing."

George nodded. "Mrs. Clare. Call her, Manners, and get Berry to help her."

Ruth had gone to her room but she was not undressed and within a minute she came hurrying down the stairs. Her astonished eyes took in the incredible scene. Jenkins and his assistant had gone back to the lodge. Sir Eustace had sunk into a chair and sat there feebly fumbling in his pockets for his pipe and tobacco pouch. His air of pompous self-importance was gone. He looked shrunken and old.

George stood by uneasily, shifting his feet, like an overgrown schoolboy caught in a fault. Julian, less over-whelmed than the others, was merely chilled and exhaust-ed by his recent efforts. Glide alone was alert as ever. All four were dishevelled, and wet with melting snow. In the midst of this sorry group the Russian kept his feet by a sheer effort of will. He was still clasping the body of the girl in his arms. They had tried to take her from him, but he resisted them with the strength of despair.

Ruth went up to him. "Let me have her. She will be safe with me," she said gently. He looked down at her, meeting that steady gaze, and his tortured face relaxed slightly.

"She is mine." His numbed lips formed the words with difficulty. "Mine. You understand. You will not let them take her away?"

"I understand," she said. "I promise."

Diana was beginning to recover consciousness, moaning and sighing and shivering in her drenched clothes. Berry, the middle-aged head housemaid, summoned by Manners, appeared on the other side, quiet and efficient, and between them they half led, half carried her away. George. Tunbridge, collecting his scattered wits, hurried after them.

"I say, Ruth, better not disturb the old lady. Take her to one of the other rooms. This'll mean a hell of a row."

"Very well, I'd thought of that."

He returned to the group by the fire. A cloud of steam was rising from them. The old butler was binding the Russian's wrist with a strip of linen while Julian was mixing them all stiff pegs of whisky. George, glancing at the clock, was surprised to see that it was only a quarter past ten.

"We'll have to talk this out," he said as he set down his empty glass, "but I'd like to change first. All of us. You too, Pavlovski. We don't want to nurse you through pneumonia."

The spirit had burnt the Russian's throat but it had done him good. His dark eyes had lost their glazed look and he answered in something approaching his normal voice. "All my clothes are in the lake."

"I can rig him out," offered Julian.

The Russian murmured a word of thanks. George looked after them as they went off together.

"I believe Julian sides with him," he thought, "the free-masonry of youth." He turned to his cousin, masking his compassion with a factitious heartiness. "Come along, Eustace, my dear fellow. Can't hang about in wet things."

Half an hour later they met again in the library.

The chauffeur remained standing. The others were seated. Julian had offered to go but Sir Eustace seemed indifferent to his presence.

"This has been a shock," he said. "I was—totally unprepared. I think an explanation is due—"

Pavlovski answered in a low voice. "I very much regret the pain we have given you. And—and the accident to the car. I don't ask for pardon. I do not expect it. I should not pardon myself in your place. But we could not help it. It began weeks ago at Cannes. I wanted her to come away with me before, but she was afraid of her grandmother, whose heart was set on her marrying you, and, also, she was afraid of being poor. And so, though she was my lover, she said no when I begged and prayed her. Enfin—tonight she came and told me that she was to be married quite soon, in two weeks, and that she could not face it. And so—it was madness—but we did not mean to steal the car. I was to leave it at Parminster."

"Thank you," said Sir Eustace simply. "That is quite clear."

"He's taking it uncommonly well," thought his cousin, "but the poor old chap is hard hit." He looked round at the others.

"We can leave it at that for tonight perhaps?"

"One moment," said Glide. He leaned forward, pointing at Pavlovski with a bony forefinger. "You and she have been meeting in secret?"

The Russian reddened angrily. He was prepared to humble himself before the man he had wronged, not before others.

"Is it your business?"

"I think so. I am here to find out, if I can, who killed Edgar Stallard. Hugh Darrow, who has been arrested tonight for the crime, swore that there were people whispering together in the gallery when he entered it. We know that you did not go to the dance with the other servants. The police have your statement. You had toothache and went to bed in your room over the garage. Was that the truth, or a lie?"

Sir Eustace did not move, but George half rose from his chair and sat down again. Where would this lead them? Pavlovski's flush had faded, leaving him pale under his tan. There was a silence.

At last he said. "I made an excuse to stay away from the dance because of Justine Dubois. I wanted to keep out of her way. I had no hope of meeting Diana, but as I stood outside the garage I saw a flash from an electric torch in one of the windows of the gallery, and I took that for a signal and went over. The garden door was open—that is to say, it was not locked—and I stepped in. Diana was there in the window embrasure we had sat in before, but she was surprised to see me and reproached me for coming because it wasn't safe. I said, 'I agree that it isn't safe, but why did you flash your torch for me?' She said 'I didn't. You must go now!' All this, you understand, was in a whisper, because we were both afraid. So I got out quickly, and Diana locked the door by which I had entered, and escaped herself by way of the music-room."

"The jade cigarette holder found among the cushions was yours?"

"Yes."

Glide tapped his thumbnail against his teeth thoughtfully. "When you saw the light did you go at once?"

"No. I had my boots on. I went up to my room and changed into rubber soled shoes."

"I see. How long would you say elapsed between your seeing that flash of light and entering the gallery?"

"It's hard to say. Three minutes. Possibly five."

"You had no idea until the following morning that a murder had been committed in the gallery either just before or just after you were there?"

"No."

"Murderers are hanged in England, Pavlovski, but there are such things as extenuating circumstances."

"I didn't kill him!" cried the Russian violently.

"No," said Glide resignedly, "I was afraid you hadn't. Your guilt would leave too many loose ends, unless, of course, one assumes that you and the young lady planned it together. It was premeditated. A note was written that brought the victim to the place appointed. The murderer crept up in the dark, flashed a torch in his face, and struck. That was the light you saw."

"I didn't kill him. I saw nothing. I knew nothing."

"But Diana said—" began George, and broke off in confusion.

Glide smiled. "You all made statements, Mr. Tunbridge. Some of them, it seems, were false."

George groaned. "Will the police have to be told all this?"

"I'm afraid so."

XV
THE PIECES SCATTERED

A TAXI STOPPED before one of the houses in the square, and an old lady dressed in black got out, waited until the driver had carried her bags up the steps, and then presented him with his exact fare. He went off, grumbling, while the harassed proprietress of the establishment opened the door.

"You're back earlier than I expected, Mrs. Storey, but very welcome, I'm sure. Mrs. Harrison and Miss Dick and Miss Watson will be glad. They haven't been able to get anyone to make a fourth. And where's Miss Storey?"

"She is staying with friends. I suppose some one will bring up my bags?"

The proprietress waited until the turn of the stairs had hidden her returning guest from view before she hurried into the drawing-room where Miss Dick sat by the fire reading a novel from the lending library round the corner.

The proprietress was excited for she had read accounts in the papers of the tragedy at Laverne Peveril, and everyone in the boarding-house was talking about it. Conversation at lunch and at dinner had been quite animated.

"Miss Dick! Mrs. Storey has come back. Alone. I didn't think she ever let that poor child out of her sight. She's staying with friends, she says. That terrible affair must have spoilt their visit. I wonder if those Tunbridges were nice to them!"

Mrs. Storey meanwhile sat down to rest in the rickety wicker chair that was wedged between her bed and her chest of drawers. In the square below the one-legged man who came round once a week was grinding a barrel organ. She recognized the tune. They had been dancing to it at Laverne one night. Diana, in white and silver, her bright hair gleaming, with one of the boys from the vicarage; Pearl Tunbridge with Stallard. The old woman closed her eyes wearily. One could not go back. What was done was done.

Presently, when the bell rang, she would go down to eat boiled mutton and turnips, with stewed prunes to follow. She would sit alone at the little table by the window. There would be the same mark of spilt gravy on the carpet. Afterwards, in the drawing-room, coffee essence would be served in chipped cups to the guests before they dispersed for the evening, some to their rooms, some to the Pictures. She would play bridge. She had nothing more to look forward to now. Nothing to hope for but something to fear. She had been spending recklessly. She might not be able to afford to stay on. For the last six months they had been living far beyond their means, and she owed a great deal of money to Colette. The bills would be sent in when the dressmaker heard the news. There would be a paragraph in the social column of the papers in a day or two.

The marriage arranged between Sir Eustace Tunbridge of Laverne Magna and Miss Diana Storey will not take place.

"After all I have done for her," she thought. "Oh, God! All my life I have been hampered by fools."

Her wrinkled hands, with their thickened arthritic joints, twitched on her lap. If the girl had been there she could scarcely have restrained herself from striking her. Physical violence would have relieved the surcharged bitterness of her heart.

The dinner bell clanged down in the basement. She got up. The black dress she had worn to travel in would do for tonight.

"I shall have to fend off these prying women," she thought as she went downstairs. It would not be difficult, for they were all a little afraid of her sharp tongue.

She stopped, smiling amiably, at several of the other tables on her way to her own.

"Did you have a nice Christmas, Miss Watson? I'm so glad. Oh, thank you. Yes, it was very unfortunate and distressing. Terrible! I can't trust myself to speak of it. No. My granddaughter is staying with friends."

Later, in the drawing-room, as they cut for partners, Miss Dick said. "Dear me! It seems now as if you'd never been away. Don't you feel that yourself?"

"I can't quite say that," said Mrs. Storey.

A little before ten she was called to the telephone. She went reluctantly for, like many women of her generation, she had never grown accustomed to the instrument and found it difficult both to hear and to make herself heard. Also, the telephone was in the passage near the front door where everything that was said could be listened to by the waitresses setting the breakfast tables and the proprietress making up the accounts in her lair.

At the other end of the wire Ruth Clare, in her private sitting-room at the Ritz, covered the receiver with her hand while she turned to summon Diana Storey. "Won't you speak to her yourself?"

"No. It wouldn't be any use. You don't know Grandma. It's no good, Mrs. Clare."

"Very well . . . hallo . . . yes, it is Mrs. Clare speaking. I brought Diana up to Town with me this afternoon. What! Oh, but surely . . . wouldn't it be wiser to make the best of it? May I come round and talk things over with you tomorrow? . . . Oh, of course I shouldn't dream of forcing myself . . . I'm sorry . . . I said I'm sorry. I hope you may change your mind, Mrs. Storey. Isn't it a pity to be so hard?"

Ruth waited a moment longer before she hung up the receiver. Her face was flushed. "Well, that's that," she said.

Diana asked no questions. Her lovely face expressed no emotion. She sat turning over the pages of an illustrated fashion paper. "There are several models here with skirts dipping at the sides," she said.

Ruth bit her lip. She was too kind-hearted to regret the impulse that had prompted her to take charge of the girl when her grandmother, on the morning after her attempted flight, refused to see her. It was obviously better that the two should be apart for a while and it was equally obvious that the Tunbridges could not be expected to extend their invitation to any of their guests. Ruth, characteristically, had thrown herself into the breach.

"I'm going back to the Ritz for a few days anyway. Diana can stay with me."

Diana had said "Thank you very much" politely but without enthusiasm. Berry had packed her clothes for her, and they had left Laverne Peveril without seeing the implacable old lady, who had sent her harassed host a message indicating that she wished to go back to London by a later train. Diana had only asked two questions on the journey. "Will Ivan be in London?" and "Shall I be able to see him?" Both having been answered in the affirmative she had sat quietly looking out of the window.

The Russian had called late the same evening. He had found a lodging with compatriots in one of the streets off Leicester Square, after a visit to Scotland Yard where his account of his movements on the night of the murder had been taken down by some other official in the absence of Inspector Purley. Ruth left him alone with Diana for ten minutes and, coming back, found her sitting on his knees.

"I suppose you are quite decided?" she said. "You're going to be married?"

Ivan had jumped up at her entrance and stood stiffly at attention. Diana clung to his arm. "As soon as we can," she said. "We can get a licence or something."

Ruth sent her off to bed and discussed the situation with the young Russian. He had charming manners and was far more grateful for what she was doing for them than Diana, but he was vague about ways and means. It seemed to Ruth that he understood motor engines, but very little else. It soon became evident that all the arrangements for their marriage would have to be made by her. Left to themselves they would have drifted quite easily into living together until the man's small savings were spent.

"He's very polite and he's very good-looking," she told Glide when he called to see her the next day, "but he's almost as stupid as she is. I must say that in the matter of brains they're well matched. They haven't enough between them to furnish a sparrow."

"Do not be too sure of that," said Glide slowly. "They are both good liars."

She looked at him, startled by his tone. "They are telling the truth now, aren't they?"

"Perhaps. Purley seems to think so. But he's made up his mind that Darrow is his man and he's a pig-headed beggar. Once the police have picked a winner they hate to change."

"Oh! I thought their statements would help him," faltered Ruth. "They corroborate his story. I've been hoping—"

"That's right," said Hermann Glide with unusual gentleness. "Go on hoping. That can't do any harm." She sighed. "Where have they taken Hugh?"

"To Brixton. I'm going to see him today. I should suggest that you engage Richard Vallance to undertake the case for the prisoner during the police court proceedings. He's clever and he takes a lot of trouble for his clients."

"You know best," she said. "Mr. Glide, have you—have you found out anything more?"

"So far," he admitted, "not a thing. But—mark this, Mrs. Clare. The police can only conduct their case against Darrow by dropping half the clues in their possession. The absence of any typewritten manuscript in Stallard's room, though he worked at his typewriter daily, is curious, but they can't fit it in with Darrow. They haven't found the weapon. I wouldn't worry too much."

But his tone lacked conviction. She realized, with a sinking heart, that he feared the worst.

"Mr. Glide, I won't ask you to jump at conclusions. I know that's no good. But—if you had to make a guess, who would you say it was killed Stallard?"

He shook his head. "I know no more than you. Give me a little more time."

XVI
WHICH OF THESE?

MY DEAR RUTH: I have had two visitors here. One, a Mr. Vallance, a solicitor, who tells me you have engaged him to look after my interests. He asked me a number of questions all of which I answered to the best of my ability, but really I have nothing to add to the evidence I gave before the coroner. I am afraid my manner then was unfortunate and I realize how damaging my tardy admission that I could see must be. In short, I am facing the fact that I haven't a dog's chance unless the actual murderer throws in his hand, which seems unlikely. Vallance thinks that I ought to plead not guilty and reserve my defence. He tried to speak hopefully and cheer me up and he seems a good chap and will, I think, do his best. The other visitor was a queer little man who sat fumbling with a lump of modelling wax and staring until I began to feel he was boring holes through my head. He certainly is a most extraordinary person. He wanted to know if I had heard any noises during the night while I was staying at Laverne Peveril. As a matter of fact I had on several occasions but I didn't think anything of it at the time. He then told me all about Miss Storey's bolting with the chauffeur. I knew nothing about it as it happened after the police took me away. Hard luck on Sir Eustace. He—Glide—seems to think they must both be called as witnesses for the defence as they were the couple I heard whispering in the gallery when I went in. The prison doctor is very interested in my eyes. He has known of two other similar cases. In one a man who had been blind for years was tricycling along a country lane when a branch of a tree that overhung the way brushed his face, and that did it. I have had time here to realize what it means to be able to see again. They let me have paper and pencils and I have been drawing a lot, principally sketches of you from memory. Vallance has promised to bring me a box of pastels next time he comes. I wish you could have been kept out of this mess, but he says the prosecution may call you to prove that I raved against Stallard to you. Otherwise I would beg you to sail home by the next boat. God bless you, Ruth.

Your grateful and devoted
HUGH.

Hermann Glide sat at the roll-top desk in his bare little office poring over a large sheet of paper covered with his fine spidery handwriting, and sipping a cup of tea, his third. Miss Briggs, his secretary, had left, reluctantly, at five.

"I do hope you're not going to sit up all night over this case, Mr. Glide."

He waved her away. "I've got to work. There isn't much time."

He had been busy all day, interviewing the prisoner at Brixton, interviewing a junior member of the publishing firm that had brought out Stallard's last three books, listening to the pungent remarks of Inspector Collier of the C. I. D. whom he had met by appointment at a tea shop in Victoria Street.

Collier had reminded him that he must not be drawn into the case. "Purley's got it in hand now. He's making a damned mess of it, but I can't help that. I mustn't interfere. I've been put on to something else, that kidnapping business in Yorkshire, and I'm off this evening."

"That's all right, Inspector," Glide had said. "I just wanted to ask if you knew how Sergeant Lane was getting on."

"Pretty bad. He's developed pneumonia," said his friend gloomily.

"Won't they want him to give evidence?"

Collier snorted. "Oh dear, no! According to Purley he's just a dunder-headed country bobby who couldn't be expected to do anything but mark time until the great man came down from the Yard."

"You don't agree?"

Collier wolfed down his second piece of cake and looked at his watch. He really was in a hurry. "Agree? Hell! Lane isn't a genius, but he's no fool. If he wasn't so modest and retiring he'd have been promoted before this. I think that he stumbled on the truth, and that the clue that led him to it was in Stallard's room. I think he made the mistake of letting it be known that he was on the right track—"

"You mean that some one tried to silence him?"

"Exactly."

"If we take that for granted," said Glide thoughtfully, "it does not exonerate Darrow."

Collier was on his way to York now, and Glide was tackling the problem in his own fashion. He had made a list of names, appending notes to each, and was reading them over, underlining a word here and there.

The document was headed:

THE MURDER AT LAVERNE PEVERIL
Time: 9 to 9.35

Hypothesis number one. The crime was committed by a burglar whose place of concealment in the gallery was accidentally discovered by Stallard. This theory has been advanced at various times by Mr. and Mrs. Tunbridge and also by Sir Eustace Tunbridge. Mrs. Tunbridge has some valuable jewellery, and, if the chauffeur's evidence can be believed, the door opening from the gallery into the yard was unlocked at first, though it was locked on the inside when Mr. Tunbridge went round the house after the murder was discovered. On the other hand, there was no sign of a struggle, and a burglar would not be likely to use a knife. The burglar is improbable, but the possibility of his existence must be borne in mind.

George Tunbridge. Was in the hall during the crucial half hour. Could he have slipped into the gallery unnoticed by his companion, Julian Haviland? Quite possible. Stallard was his wife's lover. Would this constitute a motive nowadays? Human nature does not change.

Eustace Tunbridge. Spent the time in the library. This is his own unsupported statement, but he had no reason to kill Stallard so far as we know at present.

Pearl Tunbridge. Neurotic, ill-tempered, given to making scenes. She might have killed Stallard, but I think only as the climax of a quarrel. Stallard was killed quickly and silently. She says she was in the drawing-room.

Jack, otherwise Rags Norris, Barbara Norris, Henry, otherwise Bunny Brett, Herbert Gunn, Angela Haviland. These young people hid together in the conservatory and can safely be counted out. Angela Haviland, however, overheard an important conversation between Mrs. Clare and the prisoner, and will almost certainly be called by the police as a witness to prove malice.

Joan Norris. Hid alone in the housemaid's cupboard. Had been singled out for notice by Stallard and apparently fancied herself in love with him. Very young and possibly hysterical. No motive so far as we know.

Julian Haviland. Was in the hall with Tunbridge. Lounge lizard type, but seems harmless. Disliked Stallard—but so did many other people. No adequate motive.

Mrs. Storey. Took no part in the game of hide and seek but went up to her room just before nine. No motive.

Mrs. Clare. Spent the time in the dining-room. Her statement is uncorroborated. It would have been physically possible for her to enter the gallery and stab Stallard. There was time for any of these people to conceal the weapon before the crime was discovered. It is not unheard of for a murderer to seek to avert suspicion by a great display of activity in tracking down the criminal. But no motive is apparent.

Hugh Darrow. According to Darrow's own statement he was in the gallery where the body lay for some fifteen minutes before he gave the alarm. He hated Stallard, who had driven his sister to commit suicide, and he found Stallard, twelve years later, still the universal amorist, playing one woman against another. *Nota bene.* The fatal blow could not have been struck by a blind man, but, unfortunately for him, there is no doubt that Darrow recovered his sight some time after his arrival at Laverne Peveril, and he cannot prove that the contributory shock was his finding of the body. He had one earlier when he learned that Stallard was a fellow guest. His attempt to conceal the fact that he was no longer blind until the opening of the inquest will make a very bad impression. Obviously he has the temperament of an artist, nervous and highly strung. Mrs. Clare, who is in love with him, is probably the only person who believes in his innocence. Neither the motive nor the opportunity is lacking. Query? Isn't the case against him almost too good to be true? There is the evidence of Diana Storey and the chauffeur. If they were in the gallery before Darrow entered it from the hall, when was the murder committed?

Diana Storey. The first statement of this young lady was a tissue of lies, told, however, with an intelligible reason. She was engaged to Sir Eustace and wished to conceal the fact that she was carrying on an affair with his chauffeur. Their story now corroborates Darrow's, but the fact that they lied to begin with will be made the most of by the counsel for the Crown, if he knows his business.

Ivan Pavlovski. See above.

Note: This was a murder in cold blood, planned by some one who knew about the game of hide and seek played in the dark and was prepared to take advantage of it, and this narrows the field, for only the persons named above, and possibly some of the servants, were aware of the fashion in which the evening was to be spent. The note, a fragment of which was found in the dead man's pocket, was written either by the murderer or an accomplice to ensure that the victim should be in the place chosen at the chosen time.

Glide sat for a long while frowning over what he had written before he rose, and fetching his hammock and his blankets out of the cupboard where they were kept during the day, made his preparations for the night.

XVII
THE MAN WHO KNEW TOO MUCH

"THERE NOW," said the nurse cheerfully as she screwed up her eyes to read the thermometer. "You're down to normal! Isn't that nice! Sister will be pleased and so will the doctor when he comes."

The patient grinned. "Will he? I got him fined last year for forgetting to renew his dog licence."

The nurse laughed. "I always say Sergeant Lane will have his joke. Well, you ought to be jolly with all the attention you get, hot-house grapes and I don't know what else."

"It's been very kind of Mr. Tunbridge and the ladies," said the sergeant gratefully. "How's that case going, nurse? Perhaps now my temperature's down I'll be allowed to see the papers?"

"And receive visitors if they come at the right hours," said the nurse, arranging his breakfast tray. "Look at this clotted cream. Some kind friend sent it. It'll be lovely with your porridge."

"About the case, nurse. Did they call in Scotland Yard?"

"They did. And they soon made an arrest. It was the blind man. He wasn't really blind. That came out at the inquest."

The sergeant paused in the act of swallowing a liberal mouthful of porridge and cream to stare at his nurse. "Not Darrow! How long have I been here, nurse?"

"Nearly five weeks."

"Good Lord! He'll have been brought before the Bench then?"

She nodded. "The coroner's jury brought in a verdict of murder against him. Then he came before the magistrates.

Such a crowd you never saw fighting to get into the Town Hall. He pleaded not guilty and reserved his defence, and he's to be tried when Assizes open next week. Now you get on with your breakfast."

She rustled out, leaving her patient to his reflections, which, apparently, were disturbing ones, for when the doctor came on his rounds at eleven his temperature was up again.

"Look here, doctor," he said excitedly, "can I see the Superintendent? It's about the Laverne Peveril case. I've been feeling too ill to bother, but I've got to now. They've got the wrong end of the stick. I suspected Darrow at first, but then I got on to quite another line. Surely my notes made that clear? It was simply a question of looking up those cases, the old ones, I mean, in the back files—"

The doctor's cool firm fingers were feeling his pulse. "Rambling a little," he thought. Aloud he said soothingly: "You shall see him in a day or two. Plenty of time. It's all going according to plan, Sergeant, and there's nothing for you to worry about. Now see if you can't get a nap."

When he was out of the patient's hearing he spoke to the Sister. "Go on with the bromide, and keep him quiet."

"It's visitors' day. There's a queer little man been here several times."

"Tell him he must wait a bit longer. I don't like these ups and downs."

The sergeant was popular with the hospital staff. The nurses, bicycling down the High Street on their afternoons off, had been used to see him genially directing the traffic at the crossroads and escorting timid old ladies and small children over the widest part. He had been in evidence, perspiring but good-natured, at the local flower shows and

Bank Holiday sports and carnivals. No one, however, took his brief connection with the murder mystery at Laverne Peveril very seriously especially as hitherto he had made no reference to it. It was evidently troubling him now, and the young nurse who had brought his breakfast wondered guiltily if she was responsible. He was restless during the morning but he ate a good dinner. Soon after he developed disquieting symptoms. Hermann Glide, arriving a little before five, was quick to realize that there was something wrong. The probationer who took him into a waiting-room off the central hall looked scared.

"Sergeant Lane? I don't know. I'll tell Sister, but I'm afraid it's no good today."

"It's important. It's about the Laverne Peveril case."

"Oh! He's been worrying over that. Will you wait here, please?"

He waited for some time, hearing people moving about overhead. It was growing late and the other visitors had all gone long ago. The probationer had shut the door but he had opened it again a couple of inches. He rose alertly as the doctor and the Sister came into the hall. The Sister was speaking.

"I was telling Mrs. Tunbridge yesterday how much better he was. She's been very kind and Mr. Tunbridge too, and other friends."

Glide stepped out of the waiting-room. "I beg your pardon—" he began.

The doctor started violently. "Who are you?"

"I came to visit one of the patients. Sergeant Lane—"

"I'm sorry," said the doctor curtly. His nerves were frayed by what he had just gone through. "It's quite impossible. Sergeant Lane has had a relapse. He is far too ill to see anyone."

"What's the trouble?"

"Gastric."

He was turning away impatiently but the Sister lingered. "Are you a great friend of Lane's?"

"No. I want to see him about the Laverne Peveril murder. I am getting evidence for the defence."

The doctor overheard and came back to them. "He's been bothering over that, Nurse Marshall told me. Very well. You can take him up, Sister, but for Heaven's sake don't disturb him if he's asleep. I'll be back soon."

He hurried off, and Glide followed the white-coiffed Sister up the stairs and down a passage smelling of carbolic and turpentine to the small private ward in which Sergeant Lane lay.

Another nurse seated by the bed rose as they entered. The light was heavily shaded but Glide saw at once that the patient's eyes were open and that he had heard them come in. His lips moved without sound. Glide bent over him. "Can you tell me, in a word, what you found that last day at Laverne Peveril?"

The sick man made a pitiful because unavailing effort to speak. The hands clutching the sheet twitched anxiously.

The nurse started forward but Glide waved her away. He had understood. He produced a pencil and took a card from his note case and placed the pencil between the feeble fingers.

"It's no use," whispered the Sister after a moment as the pencil slipped from Lane's grasp and rolled off the bed on to the floor, but Glide took the card with its faint scrawls and replaced it in his case. "That's quite all right," he said cheerfully. "Just what I wanted. Thank you very much, Sergeant. Everything will be o.k. now."

The dim eyes in the grey face on the pillow conveyed a message of gratitude. Glide felt the Sister plucking at his sleeve. He followed her out of the ward.

"Is he dying?"

"I'm afraid so," she said. There were tears on her cheeks. "It's been such a shock to us all. We'd got very fond of him, and he seemed so much better."

"What's wrong?"

"The doctor thinks it's a duodenal ulcer. He's suffered terribly, poor fellow, ever since three o'clock, and he's so weak now that if he has another attack—" She leaned over the stair rail to look into the hall below. "The porter is there. He'll let you out. I must go back to the patient."

Glide sat up later that night in his bedroom at the Crown studying the pathetic jumble of loops and lines and dashes that would probably be Lane's last message to his fellow men. He had struggled to say—what? From the first he had been either derided or ignored. "What can you expect of a country bobby?" or "Poor chap, he was out of his depth." Purley, the great Inspector Purley, had swept him aside majestically, assuring his superiors that he had come into the case early enough to pick up all the threads for himself. Only Collier, his friend, and one other had realized his possible importance as a factor in the problem that might never now be solved.

No use, the Sister had said, but she had not known as Glide knew that a life might hang on that blurred scrawl. A life. Because of that Glide sat on while the Abbey clock chimed hour after hour, sometimes holding the card at arm's length, sometimes peering at it through a magnifying glass, straining to bridge the gap between his subtle brain and that other fading consciousness. He was stiff, numbed with cold and aching with fatigue when, suddenly, he was able to read the writing. Five words and perfectly distinct.

"That's that!" he mumbled. With the relaxation of mental effort came an overwhelming desire to sleep. He looked at his watch. Ten minutes to five. He went to the window and drew the blind. Already the stars were paling over the black bulk of the old Town Hall across the square where, in a few days' time one of His Majesty's judges in crimson and ermine would preside over twelve good men and true, where, perhaps, the terrible words of the death sentence would be uttered. He turned back into the room and lay down on the bed. Within three minutes he was sleeping the deep sleep of bodily and mental exhaustion.

He was up soon after eight and after a hasty breakfast caught a bus that put him down at the hospital gates. The main building with its recently added annex, set among untidy shrubberies on the bleak hillside, looked cheerless enough in the grey light of the February morning. A young nurse came to the door and, in answer to his enquiry, shook her head.

"Sergeant Lane died early this morning."

He saw that she had been crying.

"This morning?"

"Yes. At a quarter to five. It's upset me. Why, at this time yesterday morning I was giving him his breakfast, and he was joking. He may not have had many friends, being unmarried and living in lodgings, but everyone who knew him liked him."

"I'm sure of that," said Glide sympathetically. "His death was unexpected, wasn't it?"

"Oh, quite. Though he'd had gastric trouble twice since he came in. Attacks of sickness, you know."

"Could he have eaten something that disagreed with him?"

"I shouldn't think so. He was on a diet."

Glide asked a few more questions. He stood at the door talking until the nurse was called away. Then he took his leave, but instead of walking straight back to the road down the gravelled drive between the overgrown laurels he took advantage of the screen they afforded to make his way round to the kitchen entrance by the path used by the tradespeople. This path, at the far end, was flanked by a row of zinc dust bins. Five of them were filled to the brim with vegetable refuse and other rubbish, and the sixth was half full. Glide who had lifted the lid of each one in turn and passed on, stopped at the sixth and looked in eagerly.

After a moment he picked out a small object which he wrapped carefully in his handkerchief before he transferred it to a pocket of his overcoat. Half an hour later he was sitting in a third class smoker on his way up to Town. His small wizened face was set in lines of anxiety. He knew what he feared, but he did not yet know enough to avert the impending blow. And so while his bright brown eyes stared unseeingly out of the window at the wintry fields, his thin fingers worked indefatigably at his lump of wax. They fashioned a face, but its features were blurred, unrecognizable, and as the train entered Waterloo he replaced the wax in his pocket without a glance.

XVIII
MISS BRIGGS DOES HER BIT

MISS BRIGGS, Glide's secretary, an earnest young woman in horn-rimmed spectacles, who attended to his correspondence, interviewed callers in his absence, and made herself generally useful, had been three years in Glide's service. He worked her hard and had come to rely more than he himself realized, on her loyalty and devotion. She was at her post when he arrived at his office.

"Mrs. Clare called this morning, Mr. Glide. I told her you'd gone down to Parminster. She's booked rooms there at the Crown for the week and she told me Mr. Vallance and Mr. Lozell would be dining with her there on Monday night. She said I was to tell you Mr. George Tunbridge is upset about her engaging a young unknown man for the defence. He offered to pay fifty-fifty if she'd brief Sleham Forsyth or Sir John Ransom."

"Easy enough to say that now," commented Glide. "We're giving Lozell his chance to make his mark. He's got brains and will do his damnedest, and the judge will give him a bit of rope on account of his inexperience, which is what we need. I hope you reassured her, Miss Briggs."

"Of course I told her that you knew best and that if you weren't interfered with you'd save Mr. Darrow."

Glide grinned. "What did she say to that?"

"She said 'That's all I want!' and I said 'You must be brave'—and she kissed me. She's a great dear, I think," said Miss Briggs, flushing at the recollection.

The little man nodded. "Yes. It's a pleasure to work for her. Now, Miss Briggs, we've very little time and I may need your help. First of all, look at this card."

She took it from him. "What are all these scratches? It looks like automatic writing."

"It isn't that," he said, "though it is a message from the dead. Can you make it out?"

She pored over it for a minute and then shook her head. "I'm afraid not."

"It's a strange thing," he said slowly, "but neither can I now. Yet there came a moment, early this morning, when I'd been puzzling over it for hours, that I read it quite easily."

"What is it?"

"Mockbeggar Hall or Tregildern case."

"What does it mean?"

"It means a bit of research work for both of us," he said briskly. "Stallard's publishers told me that his new volume was to deal with a series of criminal trials and murder mysteries which, for one reason or another, had not been much noticed at the time and were now forgotten."

"I thought murders always got a good press," said Miss Briggs.

"Yes, but there might be something even juicier happening at the same time. The Crippen case, for instance. If anything else happened while that was being reported it wouldn't have got much space. Well, I got that much out of the publishers, but no details. They didn't know any more than that. . . . Now we come to ascertained facts. Stallard had promised to deliver the goods by March and he worked while at Laverne Peveril. The maids heard him using his typewriter and noticed that his table drawer was full of papers. On the day after the murder Lane spent some time in Stallard's room. Leaving it he met Miss Haviland in the passage. She asked him how he was getting on and his reply was optimistic, imprudently so. That night the gas fire in his room was turned on. He was unconscious when they found him and he has been in hospital ever since. Inspector Collier carried on until Purley arrived. Collier searched Stallard's room and the room occupied two nights running by Lane. He found no papers of any description, and he was convinced—though he did not succeed in convincing Purley—that some pages had been torn out of Lane's notebook."

"You think that, for some reason, the typescript of Stallard's book was removed by the murderer because it contained a clue to his identity?"

Glide had taken some nuts and a banana from his desk and was munching conscientiously.

"That was Inspector Collier's theory and it is mine also. Collier is one of the few men at the Yard who does not rely entirely on material clues. The others are led by what they find, hardly ever by what they don't find. Stallard could not possibly have lived as he did on what he made by his books and a little occasional journalism, but I can't find that he had private means. I think that he fished in very muddy waters, and that in the end he caught a Tartar."

"Blackmail!" exclaimed his secretary.

"Something of the sort. Obviously the resurrection of these long-buried scandals must be very unpleasant for the families and descendants of those concerned. They might be prepared to pay to avoid publication. Yes. I fancy that if we can hark back to these two cases we may get a new and surprising light on what happened at Laverne Peveril between nine and nine-thirty-five on the evening of the twenty-second of December last."

Glide had finished his packet of pine kernels and was ready for the fray. He rose. "And now," he said, "I will take Tregildern and you can take Mockbeggar Hall. I should suggest back files of one of the more exciting Sunday papers. Take copious notes of anything you can find, come back here, and wait for me. There will be another job for you when that's done."

Night had fallen when Miss Briggs returned. She found her employer engaged in boiling a kettle for tea on the gas fire in his room. An open biscuit tin and two cups set out on his desk indicated that they were to take some refreshment together.

"Some of the biscuits are sugar covered," said Glide. "Those are for you. I got them on purpose."

Miss Briggs blushed with pleasure. "That's very kind of you, Mr. Glide."

"Not at all. Muzzle not the ox, you know. At least—that is the principle."

Miss Briggs, who, in spite of her earnest appearance, was not devoid of a sense of humour, giggled. "I certainly trod out a lot of chaff, but I got what you wanted at last. There was a perfectly ghastly scandal at a place called Mockbeggar Hall in the last year of the war. It was not at all fully reported. Evidently there was a determined effort to hush it up."

She sipped her tea and took one of the sugar-coated biscuits, which, secretly, she detested.

"Go on," he said.

"Well—the house is down in Sussex, a large place standing in its own grounds, surrounded by woods and some distance from the nearest village. It had been standing empty some time when it was taken by a Mrs. St. Clair, who was described as a widow with a family of daughters. She brought her own servants down from Town with her and entertained lavishly. Her guests were chiefly officers home on leave or convalescent. There was a good deal of talk in the neighbourhood for months before any official enquiry was made. Then, one or two military secrets leaked out and the Germans seemed to have information about some parts of our line that they could not have got in the ordinary way, and it began to be suspected that Mrs. St. Clair got hold of information and passed it on. It was decided to take action, but the authorities went about it gingerly. You see, it was not only subalterns and temporary second lieutenants who were entertained down there; red tabs and brass hats were frequent. So the raiders went camouflaged, more or less, as people from the Food Controller's office come to make sure the good lady wasn't hoarding jam. But she'd had twelve hours' notice and she'd gone with the whole tribe of daughters and the servants."

"Is that all?"

Miss Briggs looked uncomfortable. "No. The paper only hinted, but it hinted pretty strongly at—at moral corruption. It wanted to know why the police had been digging up the garden, and it called on the authorities to publish the names of officers who had frequented the place. And they printed a very queer story contributed by an airman."

"What was that?"

Miss Briggs looked down at her notes. "One of our planes was returning from the coast. It happened to be flying rather low, and the observer, looking down, was startled to see a nude woman running across a clearing in a wood. The noise of the engines prevented him from hearing anything, but he fancied she was screaming. He told the pilot and he came round and landed in a field about a mile from the spot. There was a high wall with notices warning off trespassers, but the observer climbed over and presently found the woman crouching in some undergrowth. He dosed her with brandy and wrapped her in his coat and managed somehow to get her back to the plane, and he and the pilot between them hoisted her into the cockpit and took her away. They implied that the account she gave of what had happened to her was quite unprintable."

Glide grunted. "Anything more?"

"Only a letter in the next week's issue from a high official in the Air Force declaring that the whole thing was impossible and had never happened, and suggesting that somebody had been pulling the editor's leg, printed with an editorial note saying that the story had been well authenticated but that, in the public interest, nothing further would be published."

"Dear me!" said Glide. "Not a pretty story; not a story that the persons involved in it would care to have revived. But it's all very vague."

Miss Briggs' face fell perceptibly. "Isn't it any use?"

"It may be. Another biscuit? You haven't eaten many. And then you must go home. You'll have a busy day tomorrow."

She went to the outer office to put on her hat and coat. When she looked into his room again to ask if there was nothing more she could do he was seated at his desk with his head in his hands, so lost in thought that he did not answer her "Good night."

XIX
THE TRIAL OPENS

THE PARMINSTER ASSIZES opened with the usual pictur-
esque ceremonial, the judge attending divine service at
the Abbey church, accompanied by the mayor in his robes
and the Corporation. And, on the following day, the Grand
Jury, having considered various bills of indictment submitted to them, had thrown out two but had found a true
bill in the case of Rex *versus* Hugh Darrow.

From the window of her sitting-room overlooking the
market square Ruth had seen a crowd collecting outside
the Town Hall long before the time when the public would
be admitted. She was not being called as a witness by
either side but she intended to be present and Vallance
had arranged that a seat should be reserved for her in the
well of the court where the prisoner in the dock could see
her. She had seen him for a few minutes at the close of the
police court proceedings when he had been committed for
trial and since then she had written to him daily.

"She's not a woman to do anything by halves," thought
Vallance, watching her face from a distance as the court
filled. She rose presently with the rest as the judge entered
and the buzz of talk died away, but her eyes were still fixed
on the door by which the prisoner would enter.

Darrow had been brought down from Brixton by car
and was a little late. The weeks of waiting had told on him.
He was less shabby than when he arrived at Laverne Peveril before Christmas, but his dark face was noticeably
thinner and the anxious precision with which he saluted
when he had taken his place between two warders in the
dock betrayed nervous tension. His plea of "Not guilty, my

lord!" when the time came for him to utter it was made in a voice low but distinct. During the brief ensuing pause he glanced round the court and smiled faintly as he met Ruth's eyes.

The counsel for the Crown, Sir Henry Bannister, was rising in his place.

"My lord, and ladies and gentlemen of the jury, I will outline the facts of this case, painting, as it were, a sketch of the background against which two figures will presently stand out, the figures of the murderer and his victim. A party of guests had assembled at Laverne Peveril for Christmas. On the night of the twenty-second the servants went immediately after dinner to a dance in the village. It had been settled earlier in the day that the host and hostess and their guests should appear at the meal in fancy dress and that afterwards there should be a game of hide and seek all over the house. I would ask you to note that the rules of this game and the conditions under which it was to be played were discussed during the afternoon and were known to everybody some time in advance. The electric light was turned off at the main by the host, Mr. Tunbridge, at nine o'clock, and he remained in the hall with a Mr. Haviland while the rest of the party dispersed to find hiding places. Thirty-five minutes later one of the guests—the prisoner in the dock—came out of the gallery. He was greatly agitated and was calling for light. When the lights were switched on it was seen that his hands and the sleeves of his white Pierrot costume were stained with blood. He explained that he had found the body of a man on one of the window seats in the gallery. His statement was verified. The body was that of Mr. Edgar Stallard. Mr. Tunbridge telephoned to the police. Two days later Scotland Yard was called in. From the first the prisoner had been under suspicion. Witnesses will be called to prove that he bore the deceased a grudge and that he evinced excitement and distress when he learned that they were fellow guests. But the prisoner was blind, had been blind for years, and it seemed unlikely that a blind man could have killed Edgar Stallard. The theory of the prosecution is that the murderer flashed the light of an electric torch in his victim's face and struck instantly before he could move or make any attempt to defend himself. The wound, which was inflicted by some sharp instrument, was three inches deep and penetrated the heart. Stallard was wearing a thin silk shirt open at the throat. But when the inquest was opened a strange fact came to light. In the course of his examination the prisoner admitted, he was obliged to admit, that he had recovered his sight. According to his statement he was able to see when he rushed into the hall after finding the body and he attributes the fact to the shock he had received. When asked, why in the interval that elapsed between the discovery of the body and the opening of the inquest he had allowed everyone to suppose that he was still blind his answers were confused and unsatisfactory, and I must say that this deliberate attempt to deceive is hardly likely to increase our confidence in his veracity."

The first witness for the Crown was Dr. Henshawe, the Parminster police surgeon, who had motored out to Laverne Peveril the night the crime was committed. He described the position in which the body was found and the nature of the wound.

Ruth ceased to listen for a while and leaned back in her chair. The crowded court was ill ventilated and already she had a headache. Her heart was aching too. If she had cared less she might have been more hopeful. If only Hugh had had the moral courage to proclaim the fact that he had regained his sight. Yet his reticence had been natural. He had always been shy and retiring, hating to be singled out for special notice. But strangers might not understand that. Lozell would do his best. He was on his feet now, cross-examining Dr. Henshawe.

"The deceased was killed by a clean thrust in a vital spot?"

"Yes."

"A random blow might glance off a rib or off the breast bone and inflict only a flesh wound?"

"Yes."

"One might assume some knowledge of anatomy in the person who dealt such a blow?"

"It is likely."

"There was no sign of a hand-to-hand struggle?"

"None. I should say that the deceased was taken completely by surprise."

"Could you strike such a blow in the dark?"

"Quite impossible."

"You agree with the police theory that the murderer turned the light of an electric torch on his victim and struck instantly?"

"Yes."

"Would a man who has been blind for over twelve years be likely to own a torch?"

"I should think not. I don't know."

"Thank you."

There was a slight but perceptible movement in the court as he sat down again. The pressmen, who had been writing busily, exchanged whispered comments.

"Not so bad for a beginner."

The counsel for the Crown called Inspector Purley.

Purley, looking more like a farmer or a cattle dealer than a policeman in his pepper and salt tweeds, was duly sworn.

"You are a member of the Criminal Investigation Department at New Scotland Yard?"

"Yes."

"On the twenty-fourth of December you were sent from headquarters to take charge of the Laverne Peveril case?"

"Yes."

"Will you tell His Lordship and the jury what led up to the arrest of the prisoner?"

Lozell bit his lip. This was irregular but he dared not protest. He might want some latitude himself later on and he could hardly expect it if he raised objections now. It was the judge who intervened. He was very old and looked more saurian than human, but the eyes under the heavy wrinkled lids were shrewd and not unkindly.

"I think, Sir Henry, that you had better question him in the usual manner."

"Very good, my lord. Did you get statements from members of the house party, Inspector?"

"Yes."

"They all appeared satisfactory with one exception?"

"Yes."

"You discovered that the prisoner bore the deceased a grudge. Anything else?"

"I was almost sure that he was shamming blind. The next day, when he was being examined by the coroner, he admitted that he could see. I considered that the evidence was sufficiently strong to justify an arrest."

"Thank you, Inspector."

Lozell got up. "One moment. This evidence against the prisoner. May we hear what it was exactly? He could see. That is not disputed by us. My client owes the recovery of his sight—not, in his case, an unmixed blessing—to the shock he received when he found the body, when his fingers, the sensitive fingers of the blind, came in contact with that inert mass, still warm and wet with blood. He could see after that. But there were thirteen other people in the house who all had the use of their eyes." Purley remained stolidly unmoved, waiting for a direct question.

Sir Henry, with his grim smile, remarked, "You'll be able to make a speech presently, Mr. Lozell." Lozell, who had said what he wanted to say, became business-like. "The prisoner's room was searched by the police and all his possessions examined by them?"

"That is so."

"Did they find the weapon?"

"They may have done. He had a penknife and a pair of nail scissors. The wound might have been inflicted by either."

"Were they bloodstained?"

"No."

"The police took possession of his white Pierrot costume, the fancy dress lent him for that evening by his host, Mr. George Tunbridge?"

"Yes."

"Was this costume supplied with pockets?"

"No."

"No pockets at all?"

"None."

"How do you suppose the weapon was removed from the spot where the murder was committed?"

"Possibly in his hand. Or it might have been wrapped in a bit of paper and slipped into his shoe."

"Very ingenious."

"Very. The whole thing was carefully planned."

"No doubt. And the essential pocket torch? Did he carry that in his shoe also?"

Purley reddened. He was in danger of losing his temper. "No, sir. But he wore a scarf as a belt. He might have carried it in that as far as the boot-room. He went there to wash the blood off his hands before he went upstairs to change into the suit he was wearing when the police arrived from Parminster."

"And what became of the torch after that?"

"It was in the table drawer in the boot-room. Mr. Tunbridge likes to have one kept there in case the electric light fails."

Lozell was silenced. The answer had taken the wind out of his sails. An older man would have been more successful in hiding his chagrin. He would have said something, anything to divert the attention of the jury from his tactical defeat. Lozell betrayed his inexperience by sitting down then. Sir Henry smiled. Ruth was aware of a horrible sinking sensation. Vallance and Lozell had depended, she knew, on proving that Hugh had no torch. One of their few supports was gone. Well, they must move on to the next. Sir Henry had risen to re-examine his witness.

"Was the existence and whereabouts of this torch generally known?"

"Yes. It was mentioned that night at dinner. Mr. Tunbridge has his own electric plant. Sir Eustace Tunbridge asked if it was ever out of order, and he said that it had failed twice since he had it installed, and that he now kept a torch in the boot-room which is in the passage by which one would pass through the servants' quarters to the power house."

"The prisoner was present when this conversation took place?"

"Yes."

"Thank you. I will now call Miss Angela Haviland."

Angela was looking well in the furs Pearl Tunbridge had given her for Christmas. Her small freckled face was not quite so sharp and she had gained, not in assurance, for she had always had plenty of that, but in poise. Ruth, who had placed her accurately as one of those needy hangers-on, prepared to make themselves generally useful to a rich patroness in return for board and lodging, castoff clothing, and an occasional motoring trip, wondered if it was true that she had caught Sir Eustace on the rebound.

"Now, Miss Haviland, did you, on the evening of his arrival at Laverne Peveril, happen to be standing near the prisoner while he was talking to a fellow guest, a lady who had known him years ago?"

"Yes."

"He asked this lady to tell him who was present and she mentioned Edgar Stallard?"

"Yes."

"What happened then?"

"He started violently and said 'Good God! That hound! If I'd known he was to be here I would never have come!' She said, 'Why do you hate him so?' Then he said, 'I can't talk about it. But he's not fit to live!' She said 'Hush!' and then they moved away and I didn't hear any more, but of course afterwards I couldn't help remembering and I thought perhaps I ought to tell the police."

"Quite right, Miss Haviland. It was an unpleasant duty, but a duty. Thank you."

Lozell stood up. "I am not cross-examining this witness, my lord."

The judge looked at him. "Are you calling the lady to whom the prisoner is alleged to have made these remarks?"

"No, my lord. We do not dispute the fact that they were made. They were expressions of opinion and not threats."

"I see. Then I think we may now adjourn for lunch."

The court rose as the judge, a small frail figure in his scarlet robe, passed out. Ruth stooped to pick up the bag that had slipped from her lap. When she stood up again she looked towards the dock, but the prisoner had been removed. In the crowds jostling to get out she found herself next to George Tunbridge. They had written but they had not met since she left Laverne Peveril.

She thought he looked much older but he seemed pleased to see her.

"What a brick you've been, Ruth! I can't think what Darrow would have done without you. Mind, I'll help to foot the bill. That offer stands, though I wish you'd briefed one of the big guns."

"It wasn't the money, George. Glide wanted this man. He's clever. Don't you think he's done very well so far?" she said wistfully.

George grunted. "Might have been worse. People have been wondering if he's got something up his sleeve."

Ruth forced a smile. "Wait and see. Will you come over to the Crown and lunch with me?"

"Thanks. I don't think I'd better. I've brought some grub with me and I'll eat it in the car. I'm being called later on, you know."

"How is Mrs. Tunbridge?"

"Pretty fair. Nervy. I'm taking her to Monte when this is over. Julian may come with us to drive the car and make himself generally useful. It was to have been Angela, but she's got a better job."

"Not—"

The shadow of a grin appeared on George's broad face. "Eustace. He stayed on with us, you know. Couldn't face his own staff at Laverne Magna. The re-decorating was in progress, and altogether it was pretty rotten for the poor beggar. So we've been playing bridge every night and Angela has been going round our links in the park with him. He's so sore he's hardly been outside the gates in all these weeks, but Angela has cheered him up quite a lot. She may not be pretty but she's got brains, and she knows which side her bread is buttered. Pearl isn't very pleased, but I tell her Eustace might have done much worse."

By this time they had emerged from the Town Hall and were standing in a fine falling rain on the wet cobbles of the market square.

"Don't let me keep you," he said, and they shook hands and parted.

Ruth did not feel at all inclined for lunch. The reek of roast beef and cabbage met her in the vestibule of the hotel and took away what little appetite she had. There was a telegram in the rack, addressed to her. It was from Glide and told her that he was detained in Town but hoped to arrive about eight.

The dining-room and the public bars were crowded and she felt that she was an object of interest to the groups of people gathered about the hotel entrance as she hurried through on her way to her own sitting-room upstairs. She had ordered a cup of coffee and declined anything else. At two o'clock she was back in her place in the court room. The judge came back. The jury reappeared in their box and the prisoner in his, like clockwork figures in some sinister toy. Rain pattered on the windows and ceased, and a pale gleam of wintry sunshine pierced the dust-laden air like a sword and lay for an instant on the dark head and the bowed shoulders of the man in the dock.

George Tunbridge had been called to the witness stand. He was well known to most of those present, a familiar figure at the race meetings, charity balls and flower shows of the neighbourhood, and at the quarter sessions where he sat on the bench with his fellow magistrates. Interest in the case, which was already great, had been increased by rumours of scandalous revelations still to be made, and the atmosphere of the court, crowded now to suffocation, was tense when Sir Henry rose with his customary deliberation to put his first question.

"You have known the prisoner all your life?"

"Since I was about eleven. Yes."

"You have been on familiar terms with him since then? Seeing him constantly and so on?"

George hesitated. "Well—no."

"You lost sight of him when you left your preparatory school and only met him again during the war when you were both at the same convalescent home for wounded officers at Richmond?"

"Yes."

"You neither saw nor heard of him after that until ten days before last Christmas when you met him by chance in the Strand and invited him down to Laverne Peveril?"

"That is so."

"So that you really know very little about his past or his present way of life, or his character and disposition?"

"As much as we usually know about one another," said George combatively. "I mean to say—"

"Just yes or no, if you please, Mr. Tunbridge. The counsel make the speeches here."

"I shall make one presently, Sir Henry," the judge reminded him, and checked with a wave of the hand the laughter that follows a sally from the Bench.

Sir Henry proceeded with his examination of the witness. Ruth's attention wandered. There was no need to listen. She too, had seen from the staircase, when the lights went up, the figure of Hugh Darrow by the gallery door, with the dreadful stains on his white sleeves and the front of his coat. She had heard him say, "I must get this damned stuff off my hands"—and had seen him go towards the boot-room as George hurried into the library to ring up the police. A point occurred to her. Her pale cheeks burned as she scribbled on the back of an envelope and, attracting the attention of the man sitting in front of her, succeeded in having it passed on to Vallance. He read it and passed it on to Lozell.

"One thing more," said Sir Henry at last. "Before the police arrived you made a round of the house and tried all the windows and doors?"

"Yes."

"They were all securely fastened on the inside?"

"Yes."

"The gallery has three doors. The first by which one enters it from the hall, the second at the far end communicating with the built-out music-room, and the third, halfway down it, that leads to a paved court and the drive to the stables?"

"Yes."

"Was that third door locked?"

"Yes."

"Thank you, Mr. Tunbridge. On the day after the murder did you notice any difference in the prisoner's demeanour? Did he walk more confidently and without feeling his way as a blind man naturally does?"

"I—I can't say. I didn't notice."

"He played his part well?"

"No. I tell you I wasn't noticing. I was very much upset, naturally."

"Thank you."

Lozell rose with a confident air. Actually his only object now was to spin out the time. He did not want to have to open the case for the defence until the next day. By then something fresh might have turned up. Glide, when he last called at the solicitor's office, had held out hopes. "I'm on to something," he had said, and refused to say more.

"You were at school with the prisoner, Mr. Tunbridge?"

"Yes."

"Was he of a violent and vindictive disposition?"

"Far from it. He was very good-natured."

"When you met him at Richmond did he appear to have changed for the worse?"

"No."

"He was generally liked?"

"Certainly."

"The prosecution alleges that this crime was carefully planned, and we concur. Was this game of hide and seek, played in the dark, suggested by the prisoner?"

"No."

"Can you tell the court who did suggest it?"

There was rather a long pause before Tunbridge answered.

"It was my wife or Miss Haviland. Perhaps the latter, but she wouldn't have urged it if my wife hadn't been keen."

"Isn't it rather a childish game for grown-up people to play?"

"I don't know. It was Christmas time. We thought it would be rather fun. I don't suppose any of us will want to play it again."

"During the thirty minutes that elapsed between the turning out of the lights and your starting on your search you sat by the hall fire and smoked a cigar?"

"Yes. With my feet on the fender. It was a bitterly cold night."

"Your fellow seeker, Mr. Haviland, waited by the gong at the foot of the stairs and the farther end of the hall?"

"Yes."

"Are you prepared to swear that he remained there all the time?"

"I? No. The screen was between us. I believe he was there."

"And he, of course, would be equally unable to swear that you kept your place?"

"What are you getting at?"

"I am trying to get at the truth, Mr. Tunbridge. Thank you. I have no further—I beg your pardon, there is one. Was the deceased invited to Laverne by you or by Mrs. Tunbridge?"

"It was a joint invitation."

"One of those formal things? Mr. and Mrs. Tunbridge request the pleasure—"

"No. Probably my wife said, why not come down for Christmas, and I said yes, do. Does it matter?"

"Was he a great friend of yours?"

"No. Merely an acquaintance. We had not known him long."

"Thank you, Mr. Tunbridge. That is what I wanted to get at. So that you would not be likely to know if he had enemies?"

"I knew nothing whatever about his affairs."

"When you first saw the prisoner coming out of the gallery there was blood on his hands?"

"Yes."

"Were there any stains of blood on the torch which was found subsequently in the boot-room?"

"Not to my knowledge."

The judge intervened. "I think that point had better be cleared up now. Is the torch among the exhibits in this case, Sir Henry?"

"No, my lord, but it is in the possession of the police and can be produced. There were no bloodstains on the case when found, but it is of polished metal and could be easily and quickly cleaned."

"Thank you, my lord," said Lozell. "We have now elicited the fact that the torch was clean. I have no further questions to ask this witness."

XX
THE END OF THE FIRST DAY

THE LANDLADY emerged from her glass fronted office in the vestibule as Ruth entered. Obviously she had been watching for her since the crowds coming from the Town Hall had shown that the afternoon sitting was over.

"I hope you're not too tired, ma'am? You'll be glad of a cup of tea. I'll send a tray up to your room, and if you take my advice you'll lie down till dinner time." Her soft West Country voice was warm and friendly. The old head waiter was hovering in the background. The Crown had been a posting inn and still retained its character though cars had taken the place of post chaises in its stables. The rosy-cheeked country maids conducting guests to their rooms up the winding stairs, with their carved oak balustrades black with age, and down the long passages, carried candles, and though a bathroom had been installed on each floor in deference to modern requirement the genius loci saw to it that the water was never hot. The drawbacks and discomforts, the poor light, the draughts, the inferior cooking notwithstanding, Ruth had begun after a day or two to feel a kind of affection for the place. The staff might lack the brisk mechanical efficiency attained by the employees of the vast and palatial hotels in which she had stayed in London, Paris, and New York but they were agreeably sympathetic and human. "They really are kind!"

she thought as she thanked Mrs. Winch and explained that the two gentlemen who had dined with her the evening before would be coming round later and that there would be a third person, a Mr. Glide. "Will you see that he has what he wants to eat and drink, and then send him up to my sitting-room?"

"That'll be all right, Mrs. Clare." The good-natured landlady looked after her anxiously as she dragged herself up the stairs. Her face so white and there were shadows like bruises under her eyes. "Poor thing," she said to the waiter, "she'll take it hard if the verdict is what they all say it's bound to be. Fond of him. Ah, well—"

Vallance and Lozell arrived together at eight and Glide came a few minutes later. He shook hands all round, a thing he rarely did, and they drew their chairs up to the fire.

"Well, how did it go?"

Lozell was depressed and showed it. "We haven't scored a point yet. I open the defence in the morning. I shall call the chauffeur and the girl, but there would have been time for Darrow to commit the crime after they left the gallery or before they came to it. They can't have been there more than five minutes."

Glide was looking into the red caverns in the fire and holding his narrow bony little hands out to warm them before the bars.

"Darrow wasn't the only person at Laverne Peveril with a good reason for killing Stallard. You've got to convey that to the jury by hook or by crook. Stallard was in the habit of adding to his income by doing a bit of blackmailing when he got the chance. His practice was to get hold of some more or less bygone scandal and threaten to rake it all up again in a book. The people involved were generally ready to pay to be left out. But at Laverne Peveril he got hold of somebody who either couldn't or wouldn't."

"Have you any proof of this that I can put before the court?" asked Lozell.

Silently Glide took a card from his pocketbook and handed it over. Lozell looked at it closely, shook his head, and passed it to Vallance who, with a shrug of his shoulders, gave it to Ruth.

"You can't read it?"

"No. No one could. Absolutely illegible."

"I read it," said Glide, "but it took me some time. Mockbeggar Hall or Tregildern case."

"Let me have another look!" Lozell held the paper closer to the light. "I still can't see it. Are you a handwriting expert?"

Glide shook his head. "You'll have to take my word for it. Sergeant Lane discovered something about this blackmailing business when he went through Stallard's papers and concluded that it would be necessary to look up these two cases. Obviously if he could trace a connection with any member of the house party at Laverne Peveril he'd be well on his way to discovering the murderer. Unfortunately he was so careless as to leave the gas fire turned on in his room that night and had to be removed to the hospital next day suffering from carbon monoxide poisoning. He got pneumonia on the top of that and died last week of what the house surgeon diagnosed as a duodenal ulcer."

"Poor man!" said Ruth softly.

"Purley, the man from the Yard, didn't bother about what a country bobby might have planned to do and the case took a different turn. But Collier, who was ousted from it, has always believed that Lane could have solved the mystery if he'd had a chance." After a pause he added: "Lane wrote this for me when he was dying. I've read everything that was written at the time about these two cases. I think I had better give you a brief summary of them both."

He took his lump of wax from his pocket and rolled it carefully between his palms. His bright eyes rested for a moment on Ruth's face. "I'll begin with the Tregildern affair. In eighteen-ninety-four a Dr. Tregildern took a house on the outskirts of Lembury Moor in Yorkshire. He hadn't bought a practice, but he put up a brass plate, and after a while he got a few patients. He was a married man with two children, both girls. Their means were small and they had to be very careful. They had only one servant, a young country girl who came for a few hours daily. Mrs. Tregildern, who was, apparently, a trained dispenser, helped her husband making up the medicines. They had been there several months when the doctor was taken ill very suddenly and died after a few hours. There was only one other doctor in the place and he was a very old man. He only arrived after Tregildern's death, but the wife described his symptoms, which appeared to be those of angina, and a certificate was made out. But there was a good deal of talk in the village, so much that the police took action and the body was exhumed. Analysis of the organs revealed the presence of arsenic in considerable quantities and Mrs. Tregildern was arrested and tried for the murder of her husband."

Glide paused for a moment. No one spoke and he resumed.

"In the course of the trial it transpired that Mrs. Tregildern had been visited on several occasions by a man, who always came in the absence of her husband. He was a stranger to the place, and was supposed to come by train but no one knew anything about him, and beyond the fact that he was young and dressed like a gentleman no one could furnish any description of him. It was assumed that he was Mrs. Tregildern's lover. His last visit had been paid the day before the doctor was taken ill. Nothing regarding him was to be learned from Mrs. Tregildern who pleaded not guilty and, for the rest, declined to answer. The judge summed up against her and the jury brought her in guilty but recommended her to the mercy of the court. She was sentenced to death, but the sentence was commuted to one of penal servitude for life. Many people at the time thought that she was innocent, or, at any rate, that her lover should have stood in the dock with her. Probably he would have done if the police could have found him. Was he the murderer, or an accessory? Nobody knew and nobody is likely to know after all these years. Mrs. Tregildern vanished from the sight of men. Her two children were taken by relatives, and that was the end of the story as far as Lembury Moor was concerned. I was there yesterday, but I was unlucky. The girl who had been the Tregilderns' maidservant, the only one who would be likely to remember anything useful, died a few weeks ago of influenza. Now, you see, that story provides us with ground for several interesting surmises but with nothing whatever that you, Mr. Lozell, can put before the jury tomorrow. Now I will give you the Mockbeggar Hall scandal."

"I think I recall that," said Vallance. "It was during the war, wasn't it? Week-end orgies at a country house in Sussex and a possible leakage of information to the enemy. Weren't some men high up in the Service involved as well as a lot of young officers? I seem to remember that the blaze of publicity died down very abruptly. One day the papers were full of it and the next there was nothing."

"I remember it too!" exclaimed Lozell. "Wasn't there some yarn about two chaps in an airplane going over the Sussex Downs happening to look down and see a woman—" He broke off in some confusion.

"I think," said Ruth quietly, "Mr. Glide had better tell us all he knows about it."

Glide complied. When he had done there was another pause. Ruth was the first to speak. "Is this going to help at all?"

"I'm afraid not," said Lozell, "unless we can get something more definite."

There was a heavy silence. Ruth's tired eyes filled with tears. She blinked them away. She had been crying before they came, when she was lying alone in the dark on the bed in her other room, trying to rest and get back the desperate courage she needed if she was to see this thing through. Crying had been a relief because the physical discomfort, the choking in her throat, the burning of her eyelids, had prevented her from thinking of the last glimpse she had had of Hugh in the dock when the court rose. He had looked across at her, a farewell look, and in that instant, when he was off his guard, she had seen the pain and longing in that dark face.

Vallance threw the end of his cigarette into the fire and lit another. "The Tunbridges went through the war, of course," he said tentatively.

Ruth answered in a low voice. "George was an airman. When I met him first at Richmond he was recovering after a crash. Sir Eustace is a good deal older. George told me he wasn't passed for active service and that he had a job in the War Office."

"Have you any idea who Mrs. George was before she married?"

"She was on the stage, I think."

"Yes," said Glide drily. "There are several possibles, especially if we assume that the case in point was the Mockbeggar Hall business, but it's no use guessing. I am depending on Sergeant Lane."

"But—I thought you said he died," said Ruth. "Poor man! I had no idea. I thought he was getting better."

Glide turned to her. "Mrs. Clare, everything depends on whether I can secure a certain piece of evidence. I hope to get it but I don't yet know if I shall. The witness I have in mind must be found and brought to the court tomorrow, or, at the latest, the day after, and everything that goes before must prepare the way for the appearance of this, our star turn. Now I will be quite candid with you all. If, in spite of all my efforts, I don't get this witness the defence may crumble to ruin. I don't say it will, but it may."

Lozell suppressed a movement of impatience. This fellow, he was thinking, was a charlatan. A dangerous man, in spite, or perhaps because, of his cleverness. "May one ask why?" he said.

"Because a good deal would then depend on my unsupported evidence," said Glide coolly, "and I'm not what the police would call a reliable witness."

"I didn't know you were going into the witness box," said Vallance.

"I'd rather not," Glide said, "but I'm afraid I must. You'll have to approach this case from a new angle, Mr.

Lozell. We've got to talk it over, but I don't want to tire Mrs. Clare."

"Look here," said Lozell uneasily. "There's no hocus-pocus about all this, is there? Nothing—I will be quite candid too—nothing shady? I won't stand for perjury. Glide, I warn you. I'll throw up the case."

"I didn't know there were such tender consciences in the legal profession!" sneered Glide. And then suddenly, his impish grin faded and he became oddly impressive. "We're trying to save the life of an innocent man, and, at the same time, to bring a cold-blooded, cunning, and cruel murderer to justice. The means I am employing are legitimate. I swear to that before you all. We've got to take a risk. If we don't the defence must rely on the prisoner's denial of his guilt—and God help him! It's for you to say which it is to be, here and now!"

The last vestige of colour had faded from Ruth's face, but she answered steadily. "I trust you, Mr. Glide. I am sure you will do your best I won't blame you if—if we fail."

"Thank you," he said. He looked towards the two men.

Lozell hesitated for a moment. Then he said, "Very well. I will accept your assurance."

"Then I will leave you now," Ruth said.

All three rose when she did and Vallance hurried to open the door for her. "We shall all do our utmost, Mrs. Clare," he said earnestly, "and you must rest. You're tired out."

He was a young man, and secretly inclined to be romantic, in spite of his profession, and she was a beautiful woman. He found himself wishing that he could have raised the hand she gave him to his lips. But he was afraid of appearing ridiculous, so he merely gripped the slender fingers so hard that Ruth winced involuntarily as he mumbled. "Don't worry! Good night."

He closed the door and returned to the fire, Lozell was mixing himself a stiff whisky and soda.

"I should think," he said, "that Hugh Darrow must be phenomenally unlucky at cards. Now, Glide, I'm ready for you."

Two hours later, Ruth, lying awake, heard them pass her door and go down the stairs.

XXI
THE RAT IN THE TRAP

"MY LORD, ladies and gentlemen of the jury—"

Lozell, realizing that he had pitched his voice too high, paused a moment, looking about him at the court, more crowded than ever on this second day of the trial, and resumed in a lower key. "I must beg your indulgence if I seem at any time to wander from the point at issue. My divagations will be more apparent than real. My object is to prove beyond a doubt my client's innocence of the terrible crime imputed to him. I want to begin by describing to you what actually happened at Laverne Peveril on the twenty-second of December. I want you to follow the secret drama whose first act ended in the arrest of the wrong man. The murderer, whom I will call X, had already resolved on the crime, and merely seized his opportunity. The prosecution, it seems, attach no importance to the pencilled note which was found on the dead man. It was soaked with blood, but some words were legible. We can deduce the rest. 'Nine o'clock sharp. Don't fail me.' We maintain that this note was written by the murderer. Stallard kept the assignation, and was stabbed to death. What then? X left the gallery, either by way of the door leading to the central hall or by the music-room with its spiral staircase to the upper floor, as Miss Diana Storey entered it. She was in the habit of meeting Sir Eustace Tunbridge's chauffeur in the gallery. I have here a plan of the house. From it you will see that a light flashed in any of the three windows facing towards the stable entrance could be seen from the room over the garage occupied by the chauffeur. On this night she supposed that he had gone to the dance in the village with the other servants and was surprised at his appearance. He told her he had come in answer to the usual signal. While they were whispering together they heard some sound at the end of the gallery nearest to the house. The chauffeur slipped out by the way he had come. Miss Storey locked the door after him and made her escape by way of the music-room. The sound they had heard had been made by the prisoner who, unfortunately for himself, had decided to hide in the gallery. I shall call him presently to give evidence on his own behalf and he will tell you better than I can how he made his terrible discovery. Let us, meanwhile, return to X."

Lozell paused a moment. He was feeling more confident, realizing that he had secured the attention of his audience. The utter silence of that packed room proved that.

"I think we may assume that X was badly rattled and needed a few minutes' respite before appearing before the world to play his part in this grim drama. And there was something he had to do before the alarm was given. He had to remove any papers in Stallard's room that might throw a light on his motive for committing the crime.

So far he had proceeded according to plan. His fish had swallowed the bait and been hooked. But now perhaps his nerve failed him, or the time was too short. He had probably reckoned on the body being undiscovered until some while after the end of the game. In any case he did not secure the papers he wanted then, and he was, of course, unable to do so after the alarm had been given. The police arrived and took charge. You have heard Detective Inspector Purley give his evidence but Inspector Purley did not come on the scene until two days later. The police officer in charge during those first twenty-four hours was Sergeant Lane of the Parminster constabulary. He had a constable under him, Anderson, and was accompanied by a friend, Inspector Collier, of the C.I.D. They spent that night at Laverne Peveril. The following morning the Chief Constable arrived and, at his suggestion, Inspector Collier returned to Parminster."

The judge looked up. "How was that?"

Sir Henry rose, after a brief consultation with Purley.

"Inspector Collier was on holiday, my lord, and was not officially engaged. The Chief Constable thought that his presence might prevent Sergeant Lane from getting credit for his conduct of the case. It was irregular. No blame attached to anyone, but he deprecated the irregularity."

"I see. Quite. Please go on, Mr. Lozell."

"Sergeant Lane spent the latter part of that day in an intensive examination of the room and the effects of the deceased. Later he was overheard by a housemaid telling somebody, apparently in response to an enquiry, that he was making progress and that his afternoon had not been wasted. His evening meal was brought to him on a tray in the study by the butler, who noticed that he was busy writing. He tried to telephone to his Superintendent during the evening, but the line was temporarily out of order. He retired to bed early. The following morning soon after six the housemaid passing his door noticed a strong smell of gas, and going in found the room full of it. She threw open the window and ran to fetch the butler. Sergeant Lane was lying in the bed unconscious and was subsequently removed in an ambulance to the cottage hospital. At the request of the Superintendent, who was very short-handed, several of his men being on the sick list, Inspector Collier carried on until the arrival of Inspector Purley from New Scotland Yard. Inspector Collier carried out a search of the sergeant's room and of the murdered man's room. In the latter he found a portable typewriter and part of a packet of typewriting paper, but no typescript or manuscript. The waste paper basket was empty. Nor were there any papers in the sergeant's room. My lord, we think there is sufficient evidence to justify us in assuming that X, realizing that Sergeant Lane had taken possession of Stallard's papers, entered the room that night while Lane was asleep, found and removed them, and then deliberately turned on the gas."

There was, for an instant, an irrepressible stirring and a murmur of voices in the court, but it was stilled before the ushers could cry "Silence!"

"Detective Inspector Purley arrived during the evening of the second day and Inspector Collier made his report and retired from the case. The inquest was opened the following day and my client was arrested on the capital charge. He was brought before the Bench here the week after and committed for trial, and he has been in prison ever since. Now, my lord and members of the jury, my learned friend, the counsel for the Crown, may say that in directing your attention to the suspicious circumstances attending Sergeant Lane's elimination from this case I am only saddling my unhappy client with the responsibility for another crime. I agree that the person who killed Stallard was the person who tried to kill Lane. I will go further and admit that though it would have been extremely difficult for Hugh Darrow, who had not then recovered his sight, to stab Stallard with one thrust in a vital spot, on the night of the twenty-second, he could on the night of the twenty-third, when he was no longer blind, have entered the sergeant's bedroom while he slept, robbed him of the papers and turned on the gas. He could have done that, but—mark this! he has been in prison, watched over as prisoners are, seeing his solicitor only in the presence of a warder ever since. It was, therefore, physically impossible for him to administer the arsenic which caused the death of Sergeant Lane at the Parminster cottage hospital last Tuesday!"

Sir Henry rose. "My lord, these are wild charges. I must protest. Sergeant Lane's death, which we all regret, was due to natural causes."

The judge's head was thrust forward like that of the tortoise he resembled from his carapace of wig and robe.

"I am reluctant to interfere with the conduct of the defence, Sir Henry. It would be inexcusable to bring such charges, Mr. Lozell, if you were not prepared to produce evidence in corroboration."

Lozell turned rather white but he answered steadily. "I am prepared."

The judge bowed. "The jury and I are listening." Lozell resumed. "My lord, de mortuis nil nisi bonum. Yet the truth must be told in the interests of justice, and the truth is that Edgar Stallard, known to the reading public as a prolific writer of memoirs of a certain type, was not above the practice of blackmail. His method was to select a half-forgotten scandal for publication, and then approach any person who would be injured if his or her connection with an ugly business were recalled and to offer not to publish—for a consideration."

"Can you prove this?" asked the judge.

"My lord, it would be difficult to persuade witnesses to come forward. The resulting publicity would be the very thing they paid him to avoid. The person we have agreed to call X was his latest victim. All blackmailers have to face the risk that one day they will catch in their trap not a rabbit but a rat that will turn and bite. X was a rat."

"You will have to produce some sort of evidence," said the judge.

"I shall, my lord." Lozell stopped to drink some water and took the opportunity to glance round the court. He was looking for Glide, but the little man was not there. He caught Vallance's eye. The prisoner's solicitor seemed worried. He answered Lozell's mute appeal with a slight shake of his head that meant that the essential witness had not yet been found.

Lozell resumed. "My lord, before I call my first witness I must touch on the motive for the commission of the crime alleged by the prosecution. While in Egypt in nineteen-seventeen Stallard seduced and deserted a young V.A.D. nurse, and she shot herself. She was the prisoner's half-sister. Naturally he loathed Stallard. But the idea of avenging his half-sister by murdering him, after thirteen years, never entered his head. Englishmen have many faults, but they are not vindictive. A Celt or a Latin may nurse the memory of a wrong and avenge it long afterwards, but you will search the annals of British criminal trials in vain for a record of any man who killed with vengeance as his motive."

"What do Englishmen commit murder for, Mr. Lozell?" enquired the judge.

"My lord, in nine cases out of ten, to get the insurance money."

There was a ripple of laughter in the court. The usher cried "Silence!" The judge smiled grimly. "I'm afraid you are right, Mr. Lozell. You can now add another trait. Englishmen are always quick to see a joke at their own expense."

"My lord, that is one of our saving virtues. I shall now call Hugh Darrow."

XXII
THE EVIDENCE OF THE PRISONER

HUGH WALKED quickly from the dock to the witness stand. His heart was beating fast. He was aware of faces, many faces, all turned in his direction, of a patch of scarlet against the dark panelled wood of the dais in front of him. He heard his own voice, husky and uncertain, repeating the words of the oath.

"I swear by Almighty God—the truth and nothing but the truth—"

The mist before his eyes was clearing. He saw people he knew sitting on benches in the well of the court: Diana Storey's wax doll prettiness; George Tunbridge, his broad good-humoured face flushed with the heat of the crowded court room and his big hands pulling restlessly at his gloves. Poor old George, who ought to have been tramping his fields with a gun on a day like this. A dark young man, noticeably good-looking, in a brown suit, was sitting next to Diana, and then came a prim little woman in grey, and beyond her again, sitting apart in her black silk coat with a black hat tied under her chin with strings of black lace, Diana's grandmother, very upright and wearing an air of protest.

Hugh stared at them in a puzzled fashion. He could not imagine how they were going to help him. But perhaps they were not all being called as witnesses for the defence. Some might have come merely out of curiosity like all those other people at the back of the court and in the public gallery, to watch him fighting for his life, coldly, as they might have watched a mouse swimming despairingly round and round in a pail of water.

He looked away from them, seeking Ruth. She was there, sitting where she had sat on the previous day when he had seen no one but her, her pale face framed by the big fur collar of her coat, her kind grey eyes, dark rimmed with fatigue, meeting his, with a brave smile.

"Mr. Darrow—"

Hugh started. Had Lozell been speaking before? He found himself answering questions, being taken once more through the fatal half-hour that had begun when the clock in the hall at Laverne Peveril struck nine and ended when he rushed out of the gallery with blood on his hands. At the inquest he had been irritable and had made a bad impression. He meant to do better this time, but of course Lozell was making things easy for him. The test would come when the counsel for the Crown rose to cross-examine.

"You fancied, on entering the gallery, that you heard whispering and stealthy movements?"

"Yes."

"Then there was a breath of colder air, as if a door had been opened, and a faint click that might have been the turning of a key in a lock and retreating footsteps?"

"Yes."

"Could you fix the time at all?"

"Well, I hung about the hall for some minutes before I decided to go into the gallery. In fact I remember now that the hall clock struck the quarter just before I went in. It must have been about eighteen minutes past nine."

"You sat down in one of the window alcoves and heard the gong that was struck by Mr. Haviland to indicate that he and Mr. Tunbridge were about to round up the players?"

"Yes."

"It was then that you became aware of the sound of something liquid falling drop by drop on the parquet floor in the alcove opposite to that in which you were seated?"

"Yes."

"You crossed over to investigate and, fumbling about, discovered the dead body of a man?"

"Yes."

"It was a great shock?"

"An awful shock."

"You rushed into the hall, shouting for help, and, when the lights were turned on, realized that you could see?"

"Yes."

"In the confusion that ensued there was no chance for you to tell anyone that you had recovered your sight?"

"No."

"Since then your eyes have been examined by several oculists?"

"Yes. Three came to the prison."

"And they agreed that sight lost as yours was might be restored by a shock?"

"Yes."

"Mr. Darrow, you are on oath."

"Yes."

"Did you kill Edgar Stallard in the gallery of Laverne Peveril on the night of the twenty-second of December last?"

"I did not."

"I have no further questions to ask."

Sir Henry rose. "I am sure," he said blandly, "there is a good deal of truth in what you have been telling the court, the whispering and so forth, but I suggest that it did not take you a quarter of an hour to make up your mind to leave the hall. Didn't you follow Stallard into the gallery directly the lights went out and do what you had planned to do?"

"No."

"Then, as you were about to escape, some one, whom we now know to have been Miss Storey, entered the gallery and was joined by some one who entered the house by the garden door. You waited, concealed in your alcove, until they had left, and then, realizing that there was blood on your hands and that the lights might be turned on at any minute, you decided to give the alarm?"

"No."

"Until you gave evidence at the inquest no one at Laverne Peveril knew that you had regained your sight?"

"No."

"You must have played the part of a blind man extremely well."

Hugh said nothing.

"You gained certain benefits from being blind? I mean, you had a small pension, and your woven scarves were sold through an organization?"

"I was paid for my work, just as you are paid for trying to get me hanged—only not so much." Hugh bit his lip. He had let his temper get the better of him. He should not have said that. The judge spoke to Lozell.

"You must keep your client in order."

Sir Henry had reddened, but he was smiling. "You are a man with a quick and uncontrolled temper? You showed it just now."

"I have a temper. I resented the suggestion you were making."

"What suggestion?"

"That I shammed blind to draw a pension."

"Well, I admit the possibility crossed my mind. If you could deceive a houseful of people for two days, why not for longer? But, in fact, Darrow, my suggestion is that you regained your sight, not when you found the body, but on the day of your arrival at Laverne, and that the shock that contributed to its recovery was the shock of hearing that Stallard was your fellow guest."

"No."

"Can you tell us why you did not impart the good news to anybody in the interval between the murder and the inquest? There was plenty of time and you had several opportunities. Mr. Tunbridge and Mrs. Clare were both old friends who would have listened sympathetically."

"I—I suppose I was afraid they would not believe me. I realized that I had made a mistake in not speaking at once."

"After the murder, while Mr. Tunbridge was telephoning to the police, you went to the boot-room to wash your hands?"

"Yes."

"You were alone there?"

"Yes."

"You then went up to your room and changed from your Pierrot costume into a morning suit?"

"Yes."

"You replaced the electric torch in the drawer?"

"I know nothing about any torch. I never touched it."

"We have only your word for that, the word of a self-confessed liar."

"I am telling the truth."

"Haven't you just admitted that for two days you acted a lie?"

"You can bully me as much as you like. I didn't kill Edgar Stallard."

"That concludes my cross-examination," said Sir Henry, and sat down again. There was a pause while the prisoner went back to the dock. One of the journalists at the press table whispered to his neighbour. "Sir Henry's a bit too brutal I always think."

The judge had raised his eyes to the clock on the wall.

"We will adjourn now for the luncheon interval." As on the previous day Ruth was wedged in the crowd pushing through the double doors into the entrance hall and forced to overhear the comments of the audience.

"Of course, that pretending to be blind has done for him. If he'd been innocent he wouldn't have done that. One can't help feeling sorry for him."

"His counsel is putting up a good fight."

"Obscuring the issue."

"Poor devil! He hasn't an earthly."

"Can it be true about the policeman? I mean, he couldn't have done that if it only happened last week."

"Looks as if the defence might have something up their sleeve."

"He doesn't look like a murderer."

"Don't be silly! Murderers don't have special kinds of faces."

"It's very quick. Their necks are dislocated."

Ruth, shuddering, made an effort and pushed her way through a chattering group sheltering from the rain under the arcade, and set out to cross the stone-paved market place.

Vallance joined her. "What did you think of Lozell's opening speech?"

"It was fine—but do you think they believed him?"

"Oh, we've only just started. They need a little time. We've rattled them a bit. I saw Sir Henry conferring with Purley and the Chief Constable." She sighed. "I wish Hugh hadn't got angry with that horrible man! One couldn't wonder at it, but it did no good. He isn't really bad-tempered, poor boy, but naturally his nerves are all to pieces."

"It won't hurt him in the long run," Vallance assured her with more optimism than he really felt. "Mrs. Clare, you look worn out. Can't I persuade you to rest this afternoon? I promise to send over if you are needed."

"I must be there when—when—"

He understood that she meant when the verdict was pronounced.

"That won't be until tomorrow evening at the earliest, or the day after. We have several more witnesses and then there will be the final speeches on both sides and the judge's summing up."

"Then I will rest this afternoon," she said. "You are right," she tried to smile. "I am—rather tired."

XXIII
TO WHAT END?

THE FIRST WITNESS to be called after the luncheon interval was Ivan Pavlovski. There was a craning of necks in the space at the back of the court and in the public gallery as he rose from the bench where he had been seated between Diana and Miss Berry and made his way to the witness stand, for the story of the plunge into the frozen lake of the Russian chauffeur running away with his employer's fiancée in his employer's car had got into the papers at the time. Young women in the crowd whispered ecstatically.

"Isn't he lovely!"

"He reminds me of Ramon Novarro!"

"I don't wonder at her—"

"On the twenty-second of December last you were staying at Laverne Peveril with your employer, Sir Eustace Tunbridge?"

"Yes."

"The other servants left the house at a quarter to nine and were conveyed by omnibus to the village hall where a dance was being held?"

"Yes."

"You remained behind, alleging that you had toothache. Was that your real reason?"

"No. I did not care to go."

"You were in your room over the garage when the stable clock struck nine?"

"Yes."

"What were you doing?"

"I was standing at the window smoking a cigarette."

"What then?"

"I saw a flash of light in one of the windows of the gallery."

"When was this?"

"I cannot say exactly. It might have been two or three minutes past the hour."

"What did you think it was?"

"I thought it was Miss Diana signalling to me."

"Was she in the habit of showing a light when she wanted you to come?"

"Yes."

"At that hour?"

"No."

"Later?"

"Yes."

"You were not expecting it?"

"No. I was surprised. I did not think it would be safe."

"But you went nevertheless."

The young man answered with a flash of white teeth. "Naturally."

"Did you keep her waiting?"

"I changed my boots for shoes with rubber soles. Then I had to cross the stable yard and the court beyond. I remember I had to walk carefully because the brick pavement had been washed and the frost had made it very slippery. Yes, it was perhaps five minutes from the moment I saw the light to the moment when I opened the door in the gallery."

"Miss Storey was there?"

"Yes. She was surprised at my coming. She said she had only just come in to hide and that I must go back at once. She said she had not signalled to me. I could not understand it, but I did not think about it very much."

"Did you go at once?"

"I stayed a little while, but she was always more frightened, so I left as I had come, and got back to my room and went to bed. I took the aspirin the cook had given me because I was excited and upset and wanted to sleep well, and it was not until the next morning that I knew what had happened."

"Thank you, Pavlovski."

Sir Henry got up. "One moment, Pavlovski. I suppose you have been called by the defence to corroborate the prisoner's narrative. I am not disposed to dispute the accuracy of your statements so far, but I noticed, and I have no doubt that his lordship and the jury noticed that my learned friend, the counsel for the defence, was very careful not to put a certain question which he would not have failed to ask if he had been sure of a satisfactory answer. This is it. Did you, while you were in the gallery with Miss Storey, hear a third person entering?"

"No."

"According to the evidence you have given the murder was committed at about two or three minutes past nine. When you entered the gallery five minutes later the body must have been lying behind the curtains of the alcove. So far we are agreed. But the defence says that the prisoner came in after you and after Miss Storey. We say that he was there already, concealed in the alcove facing that occupied by the murdered man. I will put my question again. Did you hear the prisoner come into the gallery?"

The Russian answered reluctantly. "I am sorry. I heard nothing. I did not know when I went out that there was anyone else in the gallery."

Sir Henry beamed at him. "Thank you. That was what I wanted. I congratulate you on the straight-forward way in which you have given your evidence."

Lozell rose to re-examine. He knew now why the prosecution had left him to call this witness. And yet, if he had not done so, he would have been twitted with having failed to bring corroboration of his client's statements.

"You said just now that though you did not understand why you had seen a mysterious light you did not think much about it. How was that?"

"When one is with a person one loves very much, monsieur, one does not think."

This was the answer Lozell had hoped for, and his smile encouraged the witness.

"Your attention was fixed on your companion and slight sounds some distance away might easily have escaped your notice?"

"Yes."

"It would not be too much to say that you were passionately absorbed in one another?"

"It would not be too much."

"You are married now?"

"Yes. We were married last week."

"Thank you. I will now call Diana Pavlovski." The Russian left the witness stand and Diana took his place. A good many people looked at Sir Eustace, who was present in court for the first time since the opening of the trial, sitting between George Tunbridge and Angela Haviland. He was leaning back, with his arms folded and his eyes directed towards the judge on the dais, and he listened to the evidence given by the girl who was to have been his wife without turning his head.

Diana answered the questions put to her in her cool precise little voice. When the lights were extinguished at nine she had gone up to her room to get a handkerchief and, coming down again, had entered the gallery, intending to hide there.

"You did not think of meeting Pavlovski?"

"Oh, no. I thought he had gone to the dance though I knew he didn't want to because Mrs. Tunbridge's French maid bothered him so. But just as I got half-way down the gallery where the door is he came in. I was frightened and angry because it wasn't safe."

"You usually met later?"

"Oh, yes. When everybody had gone to bed. I had to wait until Grandma was asleep. She had the room next to mine and there was a door between. I had to be very careful."

"He told you he had seen a light in the window?"

"Yes. I persuaded him to go at last, and then I turned the key in the lock and went upstairs by way of the music-room and the iron staircase and got back to my own room where I stopped until I heard somebody shouting downstairs."

"Thank you, Mrs. Pavlovski."

"I shall not cross-examine this witness," said Sir Henry. "I don't want to waste the time of the court. Sooner or later we may get something relevant."

Angela Haviland had left her place to sit on the bench beside Mrs. Storey. The old lady greeted her with a cold smile.

"I am so sorry for you," whispered Angela. "It was brave of you to come—"

"I should not have come, but I was summoned as a witness."

"Good gracious! What of? You had gone to bed."

"Yes. I don't know what they want of me. Hush! We must not talk."

"I call Emily Storey."

The old lady rose composedly and crossed the well of the court to the witness stand. She held herself more erect than the women of a younger generation though she leaned rather heavily on her ebony stick. Her fine wrinkled skin was faintly flushed over the cheek bones but she showed no other signs of emotion.

The judge leaned forward. "Perhaps this witness will be seated. Let a chair be brought."

"Thank you, my lord." Her voice, drier, colder, more deliberate than her granddaughter's, had the same delicate precision of utterance, and the pressmen sighed with relief. They would not have to strain their ears to hear her.

"I need not ask you if you remember the night of the twenty-second of December. You were staying at Laverne Peveril?"

"I was."

"Did you take part in the game of hide and seek?"

"Certainly not. Mr. Tunbridge told me the lights would be turned off at nine so I went up about twenty minutes earlier while they were still sitting over their coffee and cigarettes in the dining-room, and undressed and got into bed. We generally sat up rather late playing bridge and I was quite glad to be early for once."

"Did you go to sleep immediately?"

"I think I must have done, for I heard nothing unusual and it was only the following morning that I learned what had happened. My granddaughter was in the habit of closing the communicating door between her room and mine. I know why now. At the time I thought it was out of consideration for me, that I might not be disturbed."

"You had no idea of what was going on between her and the chauffeur?"

"I never dreamed of such a thing."

"On the night of the twenty-third did you leave your room at all during the hours between twelve and day-break?"

There was a perceptible interval between this question and the answer.

"Yes, I did."

"How was that, Mrs. Storey?"

"I was not sleeping so well as usual. I suppose my nerves had been upset."

"Quite. What did you do?"

"I had left a book I had been reading downstairs. I went down to fetch it."

"What was the time?"

"I really can't say. Between three and four perhaps."

"Did you see or hear anyone else moving about the house?"

Again there was a perceptible pause before Mrs. Storey replied. "Since you ask me, I did see some one at the far end of the passage on the other side of the landing."

"A man or a woman?"

"I am not sure. There was a small heavily shaded lamp burning at the top of the stairs and no other light. I did not pay much attention."

"You have not mentioned this to anybody?"

"No. It made no great impression on my mind."

"It did not occur to you to tell the police about it even when you heard that there was some doubt about how the gas fire in Sergeant Lane's room came to be turned on?"

"I never did hear that. People didn't talk about the affair to me. It was too unpleasant."

"Do you think this person who was prowling about saw you?"

"Possibly. I really couldn't say."

"Since you left Laverne you have been staying at a private hotel in Earl's Court?"

"Yes."

"That will be all, Mrs. Storey."

The judge's eyebrows went up. "Are you cross-examining, Sir Henry?"

"No, my lord."

"You accept her evidence?"

"My lord, I submit that her evidence has nothing to do with the point at issue."

The judge lifted his hand. "One moment. I think that, in the interests of justice, an appeal should be made to this person whom Mrs. Storey saw to come forward. Will he or she stand up?"

There was a tense silence. No one moved.

"Not all the house party are present in court, my lord," ventured Lozell.

"Well," for the first time the judge showed a trace of impatience, "have you any more witnesses, Mr. Lozell?"

"The defence is going flop," thought Vallance despairingly. He glanced towards the jury, but their faces told him nothing. Where was Glide? He had let them down. He remembered Ruth Clare's eyes and the haunting fear in their depths. "Thank God she isn't here!"

Lozell was turning over his notes. His hands shook slightly. Too late to draw back now.

"I call Alice Marshall."

XXIV
CREAM

"ALICE MARSHALL."

A sturdily built young woman dressed in a nurse's dark blue bonnet and cloak entered the witness box and was duly sworn.

"You are on the nursing staff at the Parminster Cottage hospital, Miss Marshall?"

"Yes."

"You remember Sergeant Lane being brought to the hospital on the twenty-fourth of December suffering from carbon monoxide poisoning?"

"Yes."

"He developed pneumonia?"

"Yes."

"Ten days ago he seemed to be on the road to a complete recovery?"

"Yes."

"He was convalescent?"

"Yes."

"He was to be allowed to get up and to receive visitors?"

"Yes."

"Did he appear to be a man with many friends?"

"Yes."

"People were kind and attentive, sending gifts of fruit and jelly and so forth?"

"Yes."

"They called, I suppose, and left messages and enquired after him?"

"Yes."

"Some of these kind friends were people well known locally?"

"Oh, yes. You see, Sergeant Lane was popular. Everyone liked him. Colonel Larcombe, the Chief Constable, called two or three times, and the Superintendent came, and Sir Eustace Tunbridge and Mr. Tunbridge. Mrs. Tunbridge came too, in her two-seater and brought some lovely flowers as well as soup jelly—"

Lozell stemmed the flow. "Just yes or no, please, Miss Marshall. Ten days ago your patient developed gastric trouble?"

"Yes."

"He seemed well in the morning and made a good breakfast, but he had hardly tasted his dinner when he complained of sickness?"

"Yes."

"He grew steadily worse, and in spite of all that could be done for him he died early the next morning?"

"Yes."

"The doctor diagnosed a duodenal ulcer and no inquest was held. Did you concur with that diagnosis, Miss Marshall?"

"It's not my place to disagree with the doctor. I thought it funny. I can't say I was satisfied."

"What did he have for breakfast?"

"Weak tea, a bowl of porridge with sugar, a bit of toast and butter."

"The same as the other patients?"

"Yes."

"Was there anything else, a little luxury sent in from outside?"

"Yes. Cream with his porridge."

"Who sent it?"

"I don't know. It came by post in one of those little round tins. There was no card with it. I remember that because he asked me. He asked if I had noticed the postmark, but I hadn't, and the paper wrapping and the label had been burned. I said you can have it with your porridge for breakfast. I was on duty the next morning and I prepared his tray myself. I scraped the cream out of the tin into a little jug and he poured it all on to his porridge. He was in good spirits and joked about it. He said he was a regular old tom cat for cream. He was always so bright. Later, when he was suffering so dreadfully"—the young nurse's voice shook—"he was very brave. He—he thanked us for trying to help him."

"Did he, on that last day of his life, have a visitor?"

"Yes."

"Had Sergeant Lane shown any wish to discuss this case?"

"Yes. He'd been too ill to care about anything, but he'd just begun to take an interest."

"He had only just heard of the arrest of Mr. Darrow?"

"Yes. I told him."

"After that did he seem worried?"

"Yes."

"The visitor was a detective, a private detective engaged by the defence?"

"Yes."

"After being kept waiting for some time was he allowed to see the patient for a few minutes?"

"Yes."

"The patient by then was past speech?"

"Yes."

"But he was conscious and apparently clear-headed?"

"Yes."

"What happened?"

"He seemed to want to write so the detective gave him a card and a pencil and he scribbled something on it."

"Did you see what he had written?"

"No."

"What happened then?"

"The detective left the ward. Sister was with the patient. She told me I might go and get a cup of tea and come back in quarter of an hour. I went down to the kitchen. While I was there I saw the detective pass the kitchen window. I wondered what he was doing and I went and peeped out of the scullery window and watched him lifting the lids of the dust bins and rooting about in the refuse."

"Did he pick something out and take it away?"

"Yes."

"Did you see what this object was?"

"No."

"Thank you, Miss Marshall."

There was a moment of silence. The interest of the court, which had slackened, was keyed up again to concert pitch. Purley was losing his air of superiority and Sir Henry betrayed a growing irritation.

"My lord, I protest against the introduction of irrelevant matter. I must decline to cross-examine the last witness. She has nothing whatever to do with the case we are here to try."

The scratching of pens had ceased. The judge, very old and very wise, looked slowly from one to the other.

"You may be right, Sir Henry. But a man's life depends on this. A great and terrible responsibility rests on my shoulders and on those of the jury. It will be for me to decide when the whole of the evidence has been laid before me what is or is not relevant and to instruct the jury accordingly. Meanwhile I am inclined to stretch a point in favour of the accused."

Sir Henry answered stiffly. "I bow to your ruling, my lord. But I should wish my protest to be placed on record."

"That will be done, Sir Henry."

"Very good, my lord."

Nurse Marshall had left the witness box. Lozell drew his gown about him. He was grateful to the judge, but there were rocks ahead.

"I call Hermann Glide."

The little man emerged from the crowd at the back of the court and stepped briskly on to the stand.

His wizened monkey face was even sallower than usual and betrayed physical fatigue, but his brown eyes sparkled with intelligence.

"You were engaged by the defence, Mr. Glide, to make investigations in this case, with a view to proving the prisoner's innocence?"

"Yes."

"As the result of your enquiries you formed the view that Sergeant Lane was on the track of the murderer when he was gassed, and that the gassing was not accidental?"

"Yes."

"You believe that there were two attempts to murder Lane, of which the second was successful, and that the author of both was the murderer of Edgar Stallard?"

"Yes."

"Until recently you had no proofs to substantiate this theory?"

"Precisely."

"When you saw Lane at the hospital he was a dying man?"

"Yes."

"He was painfully anxious to tell you something, and he did, in fact, write a few words on a card?"

"Yes."

"Was the information conveyed under such tragic circumstances helpful?"

"Yes. The writing was hardly legible but in time I deciphered it. He referred me to two bygone criminal cases."

"You assumed that there was a connection between one of these cases and a member of the Laverne house party?"

"Yes."

"And that Stallard was threatening to publish the story?"

"Yes."

The judge looked towards Lozell. "Is there anything concrete?"

Lozell took the hint. "Have you secured any evidence relating to the manner of Lane's death?"

"Yes."

"What is the nature of this evidence?"

"I found the tin that had contained the cream in a dust bin at the hospital and took it to Dr. Laverton Brose, the analyst. I have received his report and have it here. He found nearly half a grain of arsenic in the scrapings of cream round the sides of the tin. I have also traced the manageress of the dairy where the cream was purchased on Monday week and the assistant at the sub post office at which the tin was handed in for despatch later on the same day. They are both here in court and prepared to identify the sender."

The excitement in the court was now intense. Once again the ushers had to call for silence.

Sir Henry Bannister was conferring in whispers with Purley.

"I shall cross-examine this witness, my lord. Now, Mr. Glide, you have told us a very remarkable story. You are, I gather, a private enquiry agent, the kind of person who collects evidence in divorce cases and that kind of thing."

"I don't often touch that kind of case."

"Why not?"

Glide smiled. "Too easy. I like something to bite on." There was a titter, instantly suppressed.

"You have not always been an enquiry agent?"

"No."

"You have had a very varied career."

"Yes."

"You have been at various times on the music hall stage as a conjurer, and you also earned your living as a professional medium."

"I have had my ups and downs."

At this point Glide who, in the witness box, had been standing with his back turned to the doors at the far end of the court, glanced round and began to show slight, but, to a close observer, unmistakable signs of uneasiness. His smile had faded, his hands were restless, and beads of perspiration stood out on his forehead. Sir Henry, who had been somewhat shaken by the course taken by the defence, began to regain confidence.

"Have you ever been indicted for perjury?"

"No."

"You might describe yourself as a lucky man?"

"Not particularly."

"Haven't you just admitted it?"

"Well, I haven't met you before, Sir Henry."

"Thank you. Would it be fair to describe you as an adventurer?"

"It depends on what you mean by that word." Glide glanced again, anxiously, over his shoulder. He was obviously unhappy.

Purley, who had been watching him, summoned a subordinate and gave him some instructions in an undertone.

"I will not labour the point," Sir Henry was saying blandly. "The jury, as men of the world, will draw their own conclusions as to the credibility or otherwise of this witness."

Lozell half rose from his seat, hoping to improve matters by re-examining, but something in Glide's face deterred him. His heart sank. What could have happened in the last ten minutes to make the little man look like that? Could it be that there was some foundation for Sir Henry's suggestions, and that some of the material he had provided for the defence had been fabricated? Lozell glanced at the note that had been handed to him a little earlier when Glide arrived with his two fresh witnesses. Who were these women? Had he allowed himself to be mixed up in something shady at the beginning of his career?

The judge was speaking. "Are you calling any more witnesses, Mr. Lozell?"

The young barrister's lips had gone dry. He had to moisten them before he could answer. "Yes, my lord—"

Glide had completed the bad impression he had already made by the feverish haste with which he had left the witness stand. He was forcing his way now through the crowd.

"Let me pass, please. Let me pass."

But Purley's instructions had been promptly carried out and a burly policeman stationed at the door barred his way.

"You'll have to wait till the court rises."

"But other people have gone out—"

"I can't help that. You keep quiet."

"Let me out. I tell you it's urgent. It's terribly urgent," panted Glide.

A second policeman approached, shouldering his way through the intervening mass of humanity, and laid a heavy hand on the little man's arm.

XXV
THE LAST WITNESS

"I CALL Edna Burnett."

A stout woman with a broad florid face stepped into the witness box and took the oath. Lozell turned to the judge. "My lord, I ask leave for this witness to give her evidence in the form of a statement. I am not myself aware of its nature."

The judge looked at the counsel for the prosecution. "Have you any objection, Sir Henry?"

"None, my lord."

Miss Burnett beamed at the judge. "It's the best way reely," she said cosily. "What I mean is you get along quicker than being interrupted all the time. Well, you see, I'm manageress of the Fair Pastures Dairy, the branch in Budleigh Terrace, and alone in the shop at the time, and can swear to the day because it happened to be my birthday, see, and this customer, not a regular one, come in and bought ninepennyworth of cream in a tin to go by post, and tins we do stock, but not many, because there's no great demand. What I mean is in Devonshire people send cream to their friends, see, but you wouldn't expect to have cream sent you not from London, see, and a seedy looking fellow too, one of the unemployed by the look of him, and I said to him, 'It runs to cream, does it?' I'm a bit sharp like that. And he says sulky like 'I'm paying you, aren't I?' It seemed queer to me and I went to the shop door and watched him down the street and he walked round the corner, and after a minute he come back and crossed the road to the Queen's Head. And I thought to myself, 'Somebody sent you to get it and gave you the price of a pint, see.' It flashed through my mind, just like that. I'm very quick—"

"When was this, Miss Burnett?"

"Monday week."

"Thank you. You can stand down, unless my learned friend has some questions to ask."

"None whatever," said Sir Henry.

Lozell bowed. "Then I will call my last witness. Gladys Croker."

Miss Croker was tall and thin and wore horn-rimmed glasses. Unlike the previous witness she required prompting, but once started she made her statement clearly.

"I am the assistant at the sub post office in Glanville Row. It's South Kensington really. I remember somebody posting a small parcel in the afternoon on Monday week. At least there were several, three or four, and two newspapers, and he put them all down on the counter together with two half crowns and waited for the change. I might not have remembered the incident," the witness explained, "if I had not noticed that one of the parcels was addressed to Parminster. I'd read about the murder, and I was interested."

"Could you describe this person, Miss Croker?"

"He was a big man, a gentleman, rather red in the face. He had a pleasant way of speaking." There was a great stillness in the court now, a great hush.

Lozell drew a long breath. "Would you know him if you saw him again?"

"Yes."

"Have you seen him since that day?"

"Yes. I saw him just now in this court. He went out ten minutes ago. He was sitting over there." She pointed to the bench reserved for the witnesses and their friends in court.

The judge leaned forward. "Does she mean Mr. George Tunbridge?"

"I think so, my lord."

"Let him be found and brought here."

There was some bustle and confusion at the back of the court. Five minutes passed. Then the Superintendent, who had gone out, returned.

"My lord, Mr. Tunbridge drove off in his car."

"He must be called to give evidence. See that he is here tomorrow morning. Meanwhile this court is adjourned."

The judge had hardly gone out when babel broke out in the court. Lozell fought his way to the doors where he found Vallance waiting for him.

"Where's Glide?"

"Heaven knows! The police were detaining him. I persuaded them to let him go and he was off like a flash."

"We'd better go round and have a word with our client before they take him off."

Darrow had been taken from the dock to the little room at the back of the court where prisoners awaited the deliberations of the juries empanelled to try their cases. One of his warders was with him, and the other had gone to bring round the car that was to convey him back to London.

"I wish they could put me up here," he complained as he shook hands with them. "I'm not so fond of motoring. Look here, what the hell do you mean by trying to drag old George into this mess?"

"You must be patient, Darrow. We are trying to clear you. We are doing our best."

"By trotting out all this rot about old George!"

"You're a nice sort of client!" said Lozell, goaded to retort. "Don't you want us to save you?"

"Not by shoving George into the dock instead of me."

"I confess I'm surprised myself," said Lozell. There was no time for more. The second warder had returned. Darrow shook hands with them both once more. "Don't think I'm ungrateful," he said huskily, "but this is all a mistake. It'll be explained tomorrow and I shall be jolly glad for George's sake. God bless you both." He lowered his voice. "Ruth wasn't there this afternoon. Is she all right?"

"Only tired. You'll see her in the morning," they assured him.

He was hurried into the waiting car by his two warders. They watched him go.

"That's that," said Lozell. "Well, Superintendent, how are you feeling?"

"Thank God it's not my funeral!" said the Superintendent piously. "Scotland Yard are in charge. I don't see myself arresting Mr. Tunbridge on a murder charge. Mind you, I don't believe it! He's one of the best!"

"They often seem so—until they're found out," said Lozell, "But I'm bound to say that our client is of the same opinion. Still, he's bolted, hasn't he?" They bade the Superintendent good night and crossed the market place to the Crown. The landlady was in the hall, evidently lying in wait for them. "Mrs. Clare is expecting you gentlemen, I know. She had a friend dropped in to tea with her, and very nice too to have some one to cheer her up, poor dear, and the little man came in just now all of a fluster and wouldn't stop to pass the time of day nor nothing but ran up those stairs like a streak of lightning."

Ruth had ordered tea when Mrs. Storey arrived. Englishwomen, in her experience, always wanted tea, especially in moments of emotional stress. She was unprepared for the old lady's appearance, for no one had told her that she was being called as a witness for the defence, but she tried to make her welcome.

"Sit here by the fire and warm yourself. Won't you loosen your cloak? I—I hope you are going to forgive Diana, Mrs. Storey?"

"I have not a forgiving nature, Mrs. Clare. I made many sacrifices for my granddaughter and I have been ill repaid. I understand that you have befriended her. Don't expect any gratitude."

"Oh—I don't. Had the court adjourned when you left, Mrs. Storey?"

"No. I came away when I had given my evidence. The air was mephitic and I dislike crowds. I promised I would ring up the proprietress of the boarding-house where I am staying to let her know if I was returning tonight. There is a train soon after seven which I hope to catch. I wonder if you would be kind enough to telephone for me?"

"Why, of course, if you'll give me the number. The telephone is down in the hall."

Mrs. Storey had poured out her tea when Ruth returned to the sitting-room.

"I hope you will forgive me. I was afraid it might get too strong."

Both women turned, startled, as the door burst open and Glide stumbled into the room. His appearance was sufficiently alarming, for his collar had broken away from the stud, his tie had worked round under his ear, and his hair was rumpled.

Ruth went to him. "Mr. Glide, what is it? What has happened?"

His breath was coming in gasps. "I ran all the way. Will you—look out?"

She hurried over to the window. "Where? What? I don't see anything!"

He appealed to Mrs. Storey. "Would you look?"

She followed Ruth to the window and they stood there together peering out.

On the farther side of the cobbled market place the crowd that had filled the Town Hall was dispersing and motor cars were driving off one after the other into the gathering dusk. The rain had ceased, and beyond the steep tiled roofs and chimneys of the old High Street the towers of the Abbey church loomed black against the greenish pallor of the evening sky.

"I don't see anything," said Mrs. Storey coldly. She came back into the room and sat down to finish her cup of tea. "Come and drink yours while it is hot, my dear." She ignored Glide who remained standing, rather uncertainly now, between the fireplace and the door.

Ruth followed her example after a moment. She felt uncomfortable. Glide was behaving very oddly. She rather wished Mrs. Storey would leave. Perhaps the little detective had something to tell her that could not be told in the presence of a third person. She was relieved when the old lady set down her cup and drew on her gloves. It was at this moment that Vallance and Lozell arrived. Mrs. Storey shook hands with Ruth, and passed them on her way out with a slight inclination of her head.

Ruth went with her as far as the landing. When she returned to the sitting-room she found the three men waiting for her.

"Poor old thing," she said pityingly.

Glide grunted. He had refastened his collar and put his tie straight, but he was still breathing heavily. He was pale, too, and his eyes were restless. The other two men observed him anxiously.

"Why were you in such a devil of a hurry, Glide?"

"I can't tell you—yet."

"What did you expect me to see from the window?" asked Ruth.

"Nothing. That is—I had my reasons. Was Mrs. Storey going to catch a train back to London?"

"Yes."

"I think I'd like another word with her. Will you come with me, Mr. Vallance? Will you remain with Mrs. Clare, Mr. Lozell?"

"Certainly."

"Good."

Ruth protested. "But I want to hear about the trial."

"Presently. You must be patient." He reflected a moment. "It's nearly seven. What about a spot of dinner for the two of you downstairs in the dining-room? You won't mind the public dining-room for once, Mrs. Clare, when Mr. Lozell is with you? Now, at once. The fact is I rather want this room to remain as it is, untouched. I'd like to lock the door and leave the key with the policeman we shall find waiting for us in the hall. We must not linger. The last pieces of the puzzle will be falling into their places, click, click, click—"

At such moments the little man ceased to appear insignificant. The brown eyes blazed, the supple fingers twitched. The others obeyed him instinctively. Something was going to happen. They knew not what. Ruth was very white. Lozell piloted her to a table in a far corner of the hotel dining-room.

"What is it all about?"

"God knows!" he said. "But you'll feel better when you've had some soup and a glass of wine, and so shall I."

"Where are we going?" panted Vallance. His legs were longer, but he found it difficult to keep up with his extraordinary companion.

"To the station."

They passed rapidly through the booking office on to the up platform. The last up train was due in ten minutes and a pile of luggage was waiting on the trucks. A small crowd of people had gathered round the door of the first class ladies waiting-room.

A tall man in a brown tweed suit who was rather obviously a policeman in plain clothes joined Glide and Vallance.

"The party I was to follow went in there, and now they say she's taken ill."

Glide nodded. "Ring up the station for a doctor and the ambulance, and then come back to us. I want you to be present when we go to her."

The man left them. An icy wind was blowing along the platform and Vallance, shivering, turned up his coat collar. An engine on a siding was letting off steam. He wanted to ask questions but he knew he could not make himself heard. The plain-clothes detective rejoined them and made a way for them through the crowd. The waiting-room attendant, a stout elderly person in rusty black, was bending over what appeared to be a tumbled heap of clothing lying on the dusty floor. She lifted a frightened face as they approached. "She's pretty bad. I don't half like it. I fetched her a drop of brandy. I hope the doctor won't be long."

Glide, stooping, picked up an old-fashioned black velvet reticule and gave it to the man from Scotland Yard. "Better make a note of the contents," he suggested.

The other looked at him quickly. "Very well." He opened the bag gingerly and placed the objects he took from it on the table. A worn leather purse, a silver pencil case, a handkerchief smelling faintly of eau de cologne and moth balls, and a white paper packet that had been opened at one end. It was half full of a white powder.

The plain-clothes man stared at it hard before he glanced again enquiringly at Glide. No one spoke for what seemed a long time. The London train had come and gone, bearing with it the greater part of the curious crowd that had collected outside the waiting-room. Only the broad back of a porter who had been left on guard showed through the frosted glass of the door. Outside the station newsboys were crying a special edition of the Parminster *Argus*:

"Laverne Peveril Murder Case. Amazing New Disclosures."

The thing that writhed on the floor like a wounded snake could not have heard. Anguish enclosed that lost soul like a red-hot cell, hermetically sealed. It was past speech and the shriek it uttered was scarcely human.

The plain-clothes man wiped his forehead. "My God! This is awful. I wish they'd hurry with the ambulance."

"It's coming now," said Glide.

There was something inhuman, Vallance thought, about his coolness. The young solicitor was greatly agitated.

"Glide—I say—you don't suggest—"

The little man's unfathomable brown eyes met his steadily. "I told you the pieces of the puzzle were falling into place. But we can't talk here."

XXVI
A VOICE FROM THE PAST

THE FOURTH DAY of the trial opened in an atmosphere of tense expectancy. The pressmen were all agog. There had been rumours of a sensational character which no one, so far, had been able to verify. One, at least, was disproved when the court opened, and George Tunbridge stepped into the witness box.

At the sight of him the cloud of dark suspicions that had hung over him since the previous evening lifted a little. He looked grave, but not as a man might be expected to look who was in imminent danger of arrest on a capital charge, and he answered the questions that were put to him clearly and without any trace of hesitation.

"You were not present in court yesterday evening when you were called, Mr. Tunbridge. How was that?"

"I got tired. This place is horribly stuffy. I had no idea that I should be wanted. I simply got into my car and drove home."

"You had no intention of running away?"

The witness smiled. "Certainly not."

"After you left, Mr. Tunbridge, a witness gave evidence that on the afternoon of Monday week you posted several parcels at a sub office in South Kensington. Is that correct?"

"Yes."

"How was that?"

"I motored up to Town that day. I went to my tailor's and then I called at a place in Earl's Court to see Mrs. Storey. I thought I might be able to induce her to be reconciled to her granddaughter, but she was adamant. She said she was going out so I offered to give her a lift. She asked me to stop at a post office and she sat in the car while I took in several parcels and papers. I didn't notice the addresses. She gave me five shillings to pay for the postage and I gave her back the change."

"Thank you. That is quite clear. Did you gather that she had been out earlier in the day?"

"Yes. The proprietress spoke to her in the hall and said something about going out twice and not overtiring herself."

"One thing more. Do you recall the night that Sergeant Lane was gassed in his room at your house, the night of the twenty-third of December last?"

"Yes. Perfectly."

"You retired to bed at your usual hour?"

"About eleven. Yes."

"Did you leave your room later?"

"No. I remember that I didn't sleep so well as usual. I was worried and upset. But I must have got off between twelve and one, and I didn't wake until Manners, my butler, came to tell me they had found Lane unconscious and his bedroom full of gas. That was soon after six, I think."

"Thank you. I have no further questions to ask." Tunbridge looked across at Sir Henry, who shook his head, and stepped down from the stand.

Lozell glanced at his notes before he began to speak. "My lord and members of the jury, I must thank you for the patience with which you have followed the arguments of the defence. It was not enough for us to affirm the innocence of my client. The circumstances were unusual. The murder of Edgar Stallard had been very carefully planned. We do not blame the police for assuming that it was committed by the man who stands before you in the dock. He was on the spot, he had been deeply wronged by Stallard, and his lack of candour after the crime was discovered was extremely foolish and was bound to arouse suspicion. We sought for witnesses whose evidence would throw a new light on this baffling mystery. You have heard what they have to say and can draw your own conclusions. It is no part of my duty to my client to point to this person or that and say 'That is the man!' or 'That is the woman!' All I have to do here and now is to ask you to record your verdict declaring my client 'Not guilty!' I would have spoken at greater length but I understand that my learned friend, the counsel for the prosecution, has an announcement to make."

Sir Henry rose. "My lord and members of the jury, what I have to say will not take long. I have to inform the court that one of the witnesses called by the defence, Mrs. Storey, who was a guest at Laverne Peveril at the time of the murder of Edgar Stallard, was taken ill last night while waiting in the station for the London train and found to be suffering from arsenical poisoning. She was removed to the cottage hospital where she died during the night. Shortly before the end she revived sufficiently to dictate a brief statement which she signed. With your permission, my lord, I will read it to you now.

"'Stallard had found out about me and threatened to put it all in his book or tell Sir Eustace. I killed him more for Diana's sake than my own. I used my scissors. It was quite easy, but I could not leave my room after I had returned to it that night to search for and destroy the typescript he had shown me. The policeman too. I did it all. This is the truth.

EMILY TREGILDERN.'"

The judge extended his hand. "I should like to see that, Sir Henry, and it had better be passed down to the jury. Have you anything more to say on behalf of the prosecution?"

"Only, my lord, that, under the circumstances we are not pressing the case against the prisoner. The evidence against him appeared sufficient to justify his arrest at the time, and his own counsel has admitted that his conduct contributed to that end. I must say that the conduct of the defence was in some respects remarkable and I hope that it will not be held to constitute a precedent."

"You can leave that to me, Sir Henry," said the judge.

"I will, my lord."

The judge settled his glasses on his nose and surveyed the court. His summing up had been expected to take about three hours. Actually he concluded it in two hours and three-quarters. Towards the close he touched on the confession, the death-bed confession of the actual culprit.

"The signature appended to that statement conveyed more to me than it may to you," he said. "I was on circuit, I had not yet been raised to the Bench at the time of the

Tregildern case thirty-five years ago. I was not briefed for either side, but I was present in court and I have a vivid recollection of the appearance and demeanour of the prisoner in the dock. I may say now that when the witness we knew as Mrs. Storey gave evidence yesterday her voice was vaguely familiar to me. One does not often hear such precise and careful enunciation. I had noticed the same thing about Emily Tregildern. It was remarked at the time that every word she uttered could be heard distinctly all over the court. I may add that she was the wife of a country doctor, that she aided him in his dispensary, and that she was convicted of having poisoned him, possibly with the help of a lover whose identity was never established, by the administration of arsenic. The death sentence was commuted to one of life imprisonment, which, in practice, means twenty years. The trial took place in eighteen-ninety-five. She was probably released in nineteen-fifteen. Naturally enough she passed under another name."

XXVII
THE VERDICT

"NOT GUILTY."

The cheering in the court was taken up by the crowd that filled the market place from end to end as it became known that the jury had given their verdict without leaving the box and the trial was over. Men and women who three days earlier had been convinced of Hugh Darrow's guilt shouted themselves hoarse. The roar of voices was audible in the little room at the back of the court to which the prisoner, now a free man, had been taken for the last time.

He had been congratulated by his solicitor and his counsel before he left the dock. Now it was the warder's turn. Everyone wanted to shake hands with him, everyone was glad. Hugh was deeply moved by their kindness. It was almost more than he could bear after the prolonged strain of the past weeks. He was trembling, and tears poured unheeded down his thin cheeks. It did not matter. Lozell, emotional, like most great pleaders, was crying too. The judge had praised him. He had taken the first step up on the ladder of fame.

"You have to thank Glide chiefly," he said. He could afford to be generous.

"I want to. Where is he?"

"He went straight back to the hotel with the news. Mrs. Clare was waiting."

"She is waiting for you," said Vallance.

"Can we go now?"

One of the warders who had been out returned. "Better wait a bit yet, sir. The crowd hasn't dispersed yet. They mean well but you don't want to be chaired, I take it."

"Heaven forbid!"

"You can stay here, gentlemen, for the present. They'll get tired of waiting before long, especially if it starts raining."

They heard his heavy creaking footsteps going down the passage, and then the door was opened again and Glide slid round it in his noiseless fashion.

"I've been over and told her. It's all right. She understands that you'll have to dodge the crowd." He submitted to being thanked and to have his hand wrung hard by Hugh. "I've enjoyed it," he said. "It was touch and go, though. I couldn't have brought it home to her if she hadn't been so determined to finish off Lane. She had the typical poisoner's mentality. They're apt to go on and on until they get caught."

The room was furnished with a table and four chairs and a fire burned in the rusty grate. They sat round the table, all but Glide were smoking. He had brought out his beloved lump of wax and was kneading it while he talked and they listened.

"I can't think how you induced her to admit that she left her room the night Lane was gassed," said Vallance.

"Oh, that was bluff. I indicated that she'd been seen and she made up a tale that implicated George Tunbridge. She was just a little bit too clever when she got him to post the tin of cream for her, but that again is typical. Still, she was a remarkable woman. Most interesting," said Glide appreciatively.

"I suppose she must have realized when she left the court yesterday that the game was up, but I can't quite understand her poisoning herself like that," said Lozell as he lit another cigarette. "I should have thought she'd have tried to twist and double a bit longer. And why did she go over to see Mrs. Clare?"

"Why? Sheer devilry. She knew Mrs. Clare was at the back of the defence, and, to make matters worse, Mrs. Clare had befriended her granddaughter and helped her to marry her lover. Let's hope, by the way, for his sake, that she doesn't take after Grandma," said Glide. "I realized the danger. I shan't forget what I went through when those idiots wouldn't let me out to go after her. If she'd used a knife! But the other came more natural to her, and I was in time, thank the Lord."

They were all gazing at him. "What do you mean?" said Vallance.

"When I got there Mrs. Clare had just been telephoning for her. When she returned to her sitting-room the waiter had brought up the tea for two she had ordered and Mrs. Storey had filled her own cup, and placed it on a side table. She urged Mrs. Clare to fill hers and drink it while it was hot. Just then I arrived and I—well—I took a chance. I made an excuse to get them over to the window and while their backs were turned I arranged that Mrs. Clare should have the visitor's cup, and the visitor Mrs. Clare's." He paused a moment. "I'm telling you this in confidence. I shan't give this evidence at the inquest. It was the best I could do on the spur of the moment. The results were unpleasant, I admit. If I had confiscated both cups and—possibly—the milk jug, and called for the police then and there Emily Tregildern might be alive now. But—I couldn't be sure. As I say, I took a chance. And there was still enough in her reticule to kill off a regiment," he added thoughtfully. "Like Armstrong. Curious."

"My God!" muttered Hugh. He looked round him like a man just awakened from a bad dream. "Can't we go now?"

Vallance left the room and came back to report that it was raining hard and that the crowd after standing for some time under umbrellas, had finally dispersed. A minute more and Hugh was feeling the divine freshness of the night air on his face. His friends were with him crossing the market place and only left him at the door of the room where Ruth waited. He stood there for a moment, hesitating, his heart thumping against his side. Then he went in.

There was no light but the light of the fire by which she sat. He went to her and knelt, and she stooped to him with a soft murmur of indistinguishable words. He silenced her with his lips on hers, and then, with a sigh, leant his tired head against her breast. It was the most exquisite moment he had known.

XXVIII
GROOVES

ONE EVENING in May Inspector Collier of the C.I.D. was seated at a table on the terrace of the restaurant facing the Mappin terraces at the Zoo when Hermann Glide and Miss Briggs came up to an adjoining table. They had not noticed him and Collier waited discreetly until their meal was nearly over before he got up and joined them.

The little man received him affably. "Do you often come here? So do I. After the kind of people we have to meet, Inspector, the society of the Polar bears and the gnus, and even the plain but honest peccary, is refreshing. How is your big bow-wow friend?"

Collier understood him to refer to Inspector Purley. He made a grimace. "Much the same. He was a bit quieter for a while after the mess he made of the Laverne Peveril case. By the way, did you know that the estate is in the market?"

Glide turned to his secretary. "You can go and see the lions fed," he said. "Take this." He handed her a bag of nuts. "I've had all I want."

She rose obediently. "They won't care for these, Mr. Glide."

He waved her away and edged his chair nearer to Collier's. "This fine old country mansion, standing in its own well-timbered park, with farms and arable lands. Seems a pity, doesn't it?" he said, "that a place that has been in the same family for three hundred years should come to the hammer. I saw in a paper the other day that Mr. and Mrs. George Tunbridge are taking a trip round the world and will be away two years."

Collier nodded. "Sir Eustace and his wife are in Venice. Pavlovski is driving a taxi here in London, and his wife is in the chorus of that new revue at the Shaftesbury."

There was a silence. Glide stared dreamily across at the bears lumbering about in their pits.

Collier resumed. "The strangest part of the case, to my mind, knowing what I know now, was that Edgar Stallard should have been stabbed with a pair of embroidery scissors. Criminals as a class are groovy, a fact for which we, at the Yard, are grateful. There's a fellow serving a long term at Dartmoor now who was caught because he would make a meal in the houses he burgled—a meal that invariably included raspberry jam. Emily Tregildern had already committed one murder with arsenic, and it was against all the canons for her to take to another weapon."

"It would have been strange," said Glide calmly, "if she had."

"Be careful!" implored Collier. "I've got a weak heart. That's the worst of you, Glide. You always keep something up your sleeve." He dropped his jesting manner. "For God's sake, don't tell me that woman was innocent!"

"Not of Lane's death," said Glide, and saw Collier's face darken at the mention of his friend's name. "Not of the attempt on Mrs. Clare. But remember what you were saying just now. Grooves! Emily Tregildern was a poisoner. She favoured the cold-blooded indirect method."

"Well, but, hang it, man!" said Collier uneasily. "She confessed. She wrote and signed the admission of her guilt in the presence of reliable witnesses."

"Quite," said Glide, "and, talking of poetic justice, she was placed in the same private ward that Sergeant Lane had. She died in the same bed. That confession was an excellent thing for us. It saved a lot of trouble all round. When the inquest on her ended with the jury's verdict of *felo de se*, and an unspoken 'Serve her right,' we could dismiss the whole thing from our minds. Mrs. Clare—Mrs. Darrow as she now is—sent me my cheque with a very charming letter thanking me for my services, and that was that. But—between you and me, Collier, I wasn't satisfied. There was a flaw somewhere. You know how it is when you tap a glass and it doesn't ring true. So I went on thinking about it, and I went on burrowing. I had nothing to gain. It was just curiosity. Or, if you like, hating to leave a thing unfinished."

"I understand," said Collier.

The little man leaned forward eagerly. "First of all, then. Why did that old woman confess? She was full of spite and rancour against everybody who had interfered in her plans. A confession made things easier for them, and she must have realized that. On the other hand, it put a stop to further enquiries. Was she shielding somebody? Not, I am sure, Diana. The girl had let her down badly, and she had not forgiven her. Who else? The answer came pat."

"Go on," said Collier.

"When Emily Tregildern was sentenced for the murder of her husband thirty-five years ago and sent to penal servitude she had two children, a girl of thirteen and another about ten years old. When she came out of prison twenty years later, in nineteen-fifteen, to be exact, the elder one had married and there was one child—Diana. Both parents died soon after and Emily Tregildern, having changed her name, went abroad, taking her little granddaughter with her. What happened to the second daughter: Now, there's a gap here and I can't prove anything, but I think she went on the stage, and married rather well about the time of the Armistice. She would be about forty-five now."

"I get you," said Collier. "Pearl Tunbridge."

Glide nodded. "Probably she has been helping her mother with occasional presents of money for years. It was she who put her in the way of meeting Sir Eustace at Cannes. Both women were very careful. They may have corresponded but they never actually met, I fancy, until last Christmas. The secret was well kept. I think Stallard only discovered a part of it. I mean, he found out that Mrs. Storey was Emily Tregildern, but he had no idea of the relation between her and Pearl."

"Then—why did Pearl kill him—if she did?"

"She was furiously jealous of him. He was cooling off, and it was his habit to be brutal to women when he got tired of them. He spent all that last day with the little girl from the vicarage. Pearl was goaded to the pitch when one sees red. She wrote him a note to ensure that he would be in the gallery—and—you can imagine the rest. She just had self-command enough to get up to her room afterwards, wash the bloodstains from her hands and the scissors, and crawl down again to the drawing-room. When you arrived with Lane she was in a state of collapse. She's a nervy uncontrolled sort of person and everyone knew she'd cared for Stallard, so her conduct did not arouse suspicion."

"What then?"

"The next day she either admitted the truth to her mother, or the old woman guessed. Stallard had begun to put the screw on Mrs. Storey, and she knew that there must be stuff relating to the Tregildern case among his papers. She probably overheard Lane telling Miss Haviland that he had a clue. So she went into Lane's room that night, took all the papers she could find, including three pages from his notebook in which he reported his discoveries, and turned on the gas. The rest you know."

"I wonder," said Collier. "Well, the case is closed anyway. Poor Lane." He sighed, remembering a grave lately visited in a country churchyard. "What's become of your lump of wax, Glide? I've never known you expound your theories without it before."

The little man glanced down at his restless fingers unhappily. "Fancy your noticing!" he said naively. "I miss it very much. The fact is I dropped it just now by accident. A llama was passing drawing a cart full of children, and he swallowed it. But—"

He brightened up. "Miss Briggs will get me another."

"You ought to marry that girl!" said Collier.

Glide gazed at him. "Do you think she'd have me?"

"She might," said his friend. "Women are funny things."

THE END